Sayonara, Sharks

Judi Peers

SOUTH COUNTRY LIBRARY

AUG - 8 2005

James Lorimer & Company Ltd., Publishers
Toronto, 2001

0614 00132 1340

2001 Judi Peers

All rights reserved. No part of this book may be reproduced or transmitted in any form or by any means, electronic or mechanical, including photocopying, or by any information storage or retrieval system, without permission in writing from the publisher.

James Lorimer & Company Ltd. acknowledges the support of the Ontario Arts Council. We acknowledge the support of the Government of Canada through the Book Publishing Industry Development Program (BPIDP) for our publishing activities. We acknowledge the support of the Canada Council for the Arts for our publishing program.

Cover illustration: Greg Ruhl

Interior illustrations: Yoshi Aoki

Cataloguing in Publication Data

Peers, Judi, 1956–
  Sayonara, sharks

(Sports stories; 48)
ISBN 1-55028-731-1 (bound)   ISBN 1-55028-730-3 (pbk.)

I. Title. II. Series: Sports stories (Toronto, Ont); 48.

PS8581.E3928S29 2001   jC813'.54   C00-933238-3
PZ7.P43Sa 2001

James Lorimer & Company Ltd.,   Distributed in the United States by:
Publishers   Orca Book Publishers
35 Britain Street   P.O. Box 468
Toronto, Ontario   Custer, WA USA
M5A 1R7   98240–0468

Printed and bound in Canada.

Contents

For Rie and Yoshiyasu,
Masako and Yasuko,
Ayako and Yoshito.

Thank you for welcoming
my son Michael and me
into your hearts and home.

1

An Awesome Exchange

You're not going to sign up?" Ben's voice echoed the disbelief etched on his round face. "You've got to sign up. Think of all the fun we'll have."

"I … I'm not sure yet." Matt Tucker crammed a tall stack of books into the back of his locker. Both he and Ben Aoki had graduated from Queen Elizabeth Public School the previous year and now attended grade nine at Adam Scott Secondary in Peterborough, Ontario. Last year Matt had been the shorter of the two, but his slender frame now stood at least an inch above his friend.

"I thought you'd agreed," Ben blurted. "It's the chance of a lifetime. You're not still worried about the plane?"

"It's not the plane," Matt said, sweeping a thatch of sandy blond hair off his forehead and tucking it into his well-worn ball cap. "That's kinda like the shark thing. You know, how you're more likely to be killed driving to the beach than you are by being attacked by a shark. I checked the stats. You were right. It is safer in the air than on the ground." He laughed sarcastically. "Actually, it's the ground I'm worried about."

"The ground?"

"Yeah. The toilets — on the ground."

"Toilets?"

Matt sighed. "I heard Japanese toilets are just holes in the ground." He turned to face his dark-haired friend. "Your father was born in Japan. He would know. Why don't you ask him?"

"I really don't care one way or the other," Ben answered sharply, a little annoyed his friend was taking such a long time to decide. "Toilets on the ground, toilets off the ground. Toilets or no toilets, I'm going for it. We may never get another chance like this."

Queen Elizabeth Public School had been twinned with Daiichi Elementary in Japan for several years. Letters, photos and videos had all been carefully packaged and shipped the thousands of miles across the Pacific Ocean. Visits had been exchanged by a few teachers and the school principals. Now Daiichi had issued an invitation to the students in Peterborough to come to Japan. Although Matt and Ben no longer attended Queen Elizabeth, they had been a part of the cultural exchange program and their graduating class had been included. Several families from Komatsu, a small city bordering the sea of Japan, had agreed to act as billets.

Kate Crowley crossed over to the other side of the corridor. She, too, had been considering the trip. Her friends' conversation had taken an interesting turn. "Where did you hear a thing like that?" she asked. "About Japanese toilets being holes in the ground."

"At the rink last week," Matt said. "Mrs. Rye told us. She and her husband were there a few years ago. And our neighbours, the Barries, they said their dad visited a Japanese factory on a business trip. The men all peed in something that looked like an eavestrough attached to the outside wall of the building." Matt's blue eyes widened. "I don't want to pee in a rain gutter, in broad daylight, with lots of people standing around."

"I can't see that," Kate said. "I mean aren't the Japanese people, like, pretty technical? You know, computers, electronics ... all that stuff." She tossed her long auburn hair and crinkled her nose in disgust. "Why would they want to pee in a hole? Just imagine the gross things that could crawl out, maybe actually bite you."

"That can happen here in Canada, too," Ben interjected. "Something fluttered against my mom once when she used the toilet in the middle of the night. She jumped up screaming and turned on the light. A bat was flopping around on top of the water."

"That's not the same thing," Matt responded. "Stuff like that doesn't happen very often."

"Seriously," Ben persisted, "aren't you going to sign up? A chance to visit Japan and live with a family over there, to go to a Japanese school for a couple of days. All we have to do is come up with our airfare and a parent to go along with us." He grinned. "I say, '*Sayonara*, Peterborough; *Konnichiwa*, Komatsu.'"

"Ben's right," Kate nodded in agreement. "We may never get another chance like this. Japan is supposed to be really cool, with all those neat temples and gardens." She piled her hair on top of her head and spun around. "And don't you think I'd look great in a kimono?"

"Maybe we could catch some sumo wrestling?" Ben added.

Matt closed his locker and turned to face his friend once again. "It's easier for you. You're half-Japanese already. You probably eat fish and rice and that, that ..."

"Sushi?" Ben offered.

"Yeah, that's it."

"I've tried it a couple of times," Ben admitted.

"I don't like that stuff," Matt said. "And I can't imagine eating nothing but rice every day. I'd starve to death over there." He frowned as he started off down the corridor. "And what about ball tryouts? Have you thought about that? They're usually the first part of May, the same time we would be away."

"I'm sure Coach will work around it." Kate fell into step with the others. Punching Matt playfully on the arm, she continued, "Seeing how you were Most Improved Player last year." Her eyes found Ben's. "What do you think?"

Ben's eyes lowered. Like a dark cloud blocking out the warmth of the sun, a shadow seemed to cross over his entire face. He swallowed. "I might not be trying out for the Sharks this year."

2

Shark Attack Revisited

Matt lay on his bed, staring up at the glow-in-the-dark stickers on the ceiling, stroking Minou's soft fur. The fur seemed almost silver one moment, then seconds later as you brushed it the opposite way it would take on a dark grey appearance. The cat began kneading her small paws into his side, gently at first, then suddenly becoming more aggressive. Matt's mind, oblivious to the pummelling, churned rapidly, replaying the argument that had broken out on the way home from school.

"I want to try something different," Ben had said.

"Hardball's not as much fun," Matt had replied. "And the fans, they don't get into it the way they do in softball. You said so yourself. Remember?"

"But if you crack the big leagues, think of all the money you make."

"Think of all the times you'll fall asleep," Matt had retorted. "The game's too slow, with checking the runner and ..."

"Not for the catcher," Ben had interjected.

"What about the Sharks?" Matt had asked. "What about the team? We could win the whole thing this year, but we need a good catcher."

Ben did not respond and an uncomfortable silence had replaced their usual banter.

Matt pulled Minou onto his chest. How could Ben possibly think of not playing for the Sharks? They wouldn't be the Sharks without Ben as catcher. Maybe, Matt figured, if he agreed to go to Japan, Ben might agree to play softball.

Unfortunately, Matt just wasn't that excited about the whole Japan thing. Not like the others were. To be completely honest, he was a little scared. He furrowed his brow and looked Minou squarely in the eye. What exactly was he afraid of?

The cat stared up at him, her yellow, marblelike eyes shining brightly, one ear twitching.

"You're no help," Matt muttered. It wasn't the plane anymore. Kim, his mom's travel agent friend, had reassured him about that. Sure, the toilet thing bothered him a bit, but not enough to keep him home. And, like Kate had said, Coach Leahy would probably work tryouts around the trip.

Was it because he wasn't quite sure what to expect? Was it the uncertainty that scared him? And the fact that it was so far away? And Japan was supposed to be really crowded, wasn't it? He didn't like it when he went places where hordes of people were rushing around. The pushing and jostling always made him feel uncomfortable.

Matt's gaze fell onto the Shark poster on the wall. There might be a lot of sharks in Japan, he suddenly realized. That would be one good reason to go. He had seen an article about the great white in a magazine at Dr. Farlow's dentist office. It showed how many sharks were found around several islands in the Pacific. At the time, though, he hadn't known which island was Japan. With any luck, it would be shark-infested.

He was afraid to go to Japan but he wasn't afraid of sharks. Did that make any sense?

Matt's interest in sharks had peaked the previous spring when his rep softball team, the East City Sharks had made a run for the county championship. The team had taken its name from the portion of Peterborough located on the east side of the Otonabee River.

Matt was the centre fielder and he had embraced the Shark aspect of the team name wholeheartedly. His major science project that year was entitled "The Amazing World of Sharks." It was the best project he had ever handed in. Ben usually got higher marks than him, but that time it was the other way around. Matt's mark was an A+.

Later, Matt applied his research material to the team, giving each player a shark nickname. Mike Freeburn became the Great White because he was tall, blond and powerful. Kate was the Fox shark, because her red hair flowed like a fox's tail through the back of her ball cap. Matt was nicknamed Megamouth; Ben, the Hammerhead.

Matt's enthusiasm had been contagious. The team had worn shark-tooth necklaces and made up shark cheers. As he lay there a couple of the cheers charged into his mind.

> Shark Attack!
> Shark Attack!
> You just can't beat
> The red, white and black!

Then,

> S ... H ... A ... R ... K!
> Sharks are gonna win today!

The East City Sharks had even agreed to eat shark steak the morning of the championship game against the Lakefield Lions. Matt's mom had barbecued the steaks for them. Matt had been the brave one that day, he remembered, the first one to try the shark. It had reminded him of tuna. Everyone had thought it was a great idea — for the entire team to become part shark for the day. His father had even videotaped them.

Matt's sigh was audible. Some team they would have this year. How could the Hammerhead shark, the team's number one catcher and one of the top batters, not play? To make matters worse, he was planning on trying out for the local hardball squad.

3

Spring Fever

For the first time since Matt could remember, the first day of spring actually felt springlike. The warmth of the sun was invigorating. Birds were chirping and squirrels were scampering about in the branches of nearby trees. Matt had ditched his winter jacket, now that almost all the snow had disappeared. It was already gone, he noted, from the green space below the old Board of Education offices where he and Ben often tossed a ball around.

Although Matt had been trying to ignore the ball issue over the last couple of weeks, he knew it would resurface soon. Spring had definitely sprung and that had always meant one thing to Matt Tucker and Ben Aoki — the beginning of softball season. Matt pushed all negative thoughts out of his mind as he cut across the field on his way to Adam Scott Secondary. Something good was bound to happen on a day like today.

"Want to get together for a game of catch after school?" Matt called to Ben, who was already making his way toward homeroom. It would be good to get the arms loosened up, Matt figured, and with any luck he could talk some sense into his friend.

"Sure," Ben replied, before disappearing through the door.

"Meet me out back then," Matt cried. "Right after school."

* * *

Matt paced back and forth on the narrow stretch of sidewalk at the rear of the school. He checked his watch again and frowned. It was almost quarter to four and school ended just after three. Initially, he hadn't worried about the passing time. He had been busy thinking how he might persuade Ben to give up the crazy idea of going out for hardball. Surely, once they began throwing the ball around and rehashing the events of last season, Ben would come around. But where was he?"

Suddenly, the back door of the gym flew open. Matt's eyes lit up expectantly. This was bound to be his friend.

Ryan Byrd, Steve Hutton and Mike Freeburn barged through the doorway, laughing and talking noisily.

"Have you seen Ben?" Matt asked.

"Didn't you hear?" Steve Hutton replied. "It's big news in science class."

"Hear what?"

Ryan, the shortstop, and Thresher shark on the team, stepped forward and slapped Matt sharply on the back. "Looks like Ben's got a thing for Kate," he exclaimed. "He asked her to go to a movie tonight. They went off together right after school."

"Oh, yeah," Matt stammered. "Right, I forgot." He didn't want the others to think he was the only one left in the dark or, for that matter, to know that Ben had left him standing waiting for almost an hour.

Steve draped one arm casually over Matt's shoulders. "Matt buddy, looks like we'll be seeing a lot more of you." Steve patrolled second base for the East City Sharks and had been nicknamed the Speckled Cat shark — Scat for short — because of a sprinkling of freckles and his catlike agility.

Matt quickly forced a smile onto his face and fell into step with the others. He was unusually quiet as the group meandered through the parking lot to the street below. This wasn't like Ben at all. He was supposed to be the reliable one. Why hadn't he told him what was up? It was bad enough Ben was planning on leaving the Sharks, but now this. Some best friend he was turning out to be!

4

You'll Have a Ball

The ringing of the phone startled both Matt and Minou. Claws extended, the cat dug her paws into Matt's side. He winced and fumbled with the receiver on the floor beside his bed. Who was calling so early on a Saturday morning?

"I'm sorry," Ben blurted. "I forgot all about meeting you after school until late last night. By then it was too late to call." He continued excitedly, "I finally got the guts to ask Kate out. Can you believe it? We ended up going to the movies."

"I heard," Matt responded bluntly.

"Are you going to the information meeting this afternoon?" Ben asked. "About the Japan trip."

"I'm still thinking about it." Matt's voice lacked its usual warmth and friendliness. "Maybe I'll see you there." He abruptly ended the conversation.

* * *

The parking lot was half-full when Matt and his mom arrived at Queen Elizabeth School, a medium-sized, red-brick building located a few blocks north of the Tuckers' home. Best friends since grade one, Matt and Ben were used to meeting at the corner of Barnardo and Wolsely. Today, however, they came separately with their parents. Just as well, Matt figured.

He was planning on giving Ben the cold shoulder to let him know how upset he was.

A large group was gathered in the school library where a colourful map of Japan graced the wall. Paintings of cherry blossoms, kimonos, carp, origami cranes, as well as photos and letters from Daiichi students, adorned the nearby bulletin boards.

Matt's eyes darted about the room. Ben was there, sitting with both parents. Matt quickly turned away when he saw him glance in his direction. Kate and her dad were sitting beside Ben. Steve, Ryan and Mike were there too. It was incredible how many of the Sharks had once attended Queen Elizabeth.

At the front of the room, the overhead projector was humming noisily, like an old, overworked refrigerator. A prospective itinerary was glowing on the wall behind Mrs. Bartley, the school principal.

Matt barely paid attention while she talked about how marvelous the Japanese people were, how beautiful, safe and hygenic the country was, and how incredible the whole experience would be. As far as Matt was concerned, it didn't really matter. He probably wouldn't be going anyway.

Matt gasped at a nudge in the ribs from his mother.

"Sit up," she whispered. "Pay attention."

"You'll need a light jacket this time of year," the principal was saying. "Casual clothes, good comfortable shoes for sightseeing, a couple of good outfits for more formal occasions, and yes ..." She tossed her long dark hair and laughed heartily. "You'll want to make sure you've got good socks. The Japanese don't appreciate holes in your socks." She waited for the laughter to die down. "Slippers are good to have too," she added, pointing to her feet. "You'll be taking your shoes off a lot in Japan. Near the front door of the school, you'll see row upon row of little cubicles that are used just for storing shoes."

Mrs. Bartley quickly scanned the audience. "I notice there are quite a few ball players here tonight. You might want to throw in your ball gloves. I've heard ball is pretty big over there."

Kate Crowley's father raised his hand. "You're right about that. The New York Mets and the Chicago Cubs opened the major league's 2000 season at the Tokyo Dome. Each team had played exhibition games against two of Japan's most popular clubs — the Yomiuri Giants and the Seibu Lions."

Matt winced at the mention of the name Lions.

"There've even been a few all-star games between our North American major leaguers and the Japanese all-stars," Mr. Crowley added.

"Who won?" Mr. Hutton asked.

"I'm pretty sure it was a tie this year."

"Long way to go for a tie," someone at the back of the room interjected.

"I've read that the Japanese love the home run ball," Mr. Crowley continued. "Needless to say, Sammy Sosa was a big hit over there."

A few members of the audience snickered at the unintentional pun.

"Needless to say," Matt's mom whispered quietly to Matt, "Mr. Crowley loves to talk baseball."

The principal was thoughtfully rubbing her chin. "I've just had an awesome idea," she exclaimed. Her eyes gleamed and her dangling earrings jingled as her arms began slicing the air. "We've always had a lot of good ball players here at Queen Elizabeth. Maybe Daiichi has a ball team. If enough kids with an interest in baseball sign up for the exchange, we could organize some sort of international challenge."

A buzz of excitement broke out among the students.

Matt leaned forward in his chair, blue eyes dancing. Playing ball in Japan. Now they were talking. "If we're going to play ball over there, I'll definitely be going," he announced.

Marg Tucker smiled approvingly. She had been urging her son to go, but maintained that it was his decision. Her face radiated happiness at his change of heart.

Matt looked in Ben's direction. He wanted to catch his eye and convey the good news. He, Matt Tucker, was going to Japan!

Ben was having a discussion with Kate. Matt waited. And waited. And waited some more. Surely his friend would look his way any minute now. Ben knew how much ball meant to him. But Kate's and Ben's fathers turned and joined in, all four becoming deeply engrossed in conversation.

Matt's head lowered and his shoulders drooped in disappointment. He listened to the rest of the presentation, signed up for the trip, then quickly left the room. If Ben was going to be such a jerk about this whole thing — fine. He wasn't going to give in either.

5

Sayonara

During the next few weeks, Steve Hutton's prediction proved itself correct. Ben and Kate spent an incredible amount of time together, hanging out after school, talking on the phone, occasionally going out. Matt spent more and more of his time with Ryan, Steve and Mike. They shot hoops on the driveway at Matt's house or at the YMCA, watched television and played video games in Ryan's basement, even did homework together.

Matt and Ben spoke to each other occasionally, but the easygoing comraderie they had always shared was slipping away. Their conversations had become merely an exchange of information. It felt awkward to Matt, forced.

"The hardball coach said he'd hold off making final cuts until I get back," Ben stated matter-of-factly.

"Coach Leahy's going to begin tryouts a little early this year," Matt responded. "He knows a lot of us are going to Japan." He did his best to ignore the feeling of heaviness that seemed to descend whenever he and Ben talked. And even that was becoming less and less frequent with each passing week.

Occasionally, Matt would wake up in the middle of the night, his mind a dusty web of jumbled thoughts. He wished he could press "rewind" and back things up a bit. He had been the jerk; he realized that now. Ben had simply forgotten about meeting him. And would Ben and Kate have even started "going out" if he hadn't given Ben such a hard time about "going out" for hardball? He knew Ben kind of liked Kate, but he had never imagined him getting so serious, so fast.

As he lay in the dark under the warmth of his cozy down-filled covers, it seemed simple. He would apologize to Ben. That would solve everything. By the time he got to school, however, he just couldn't bring himself to do it. He was glad the other guys were going on the trip. With Steve, Mike and Ryan along, at least he would have someone to hang out with.

* * *

Coach Leahy had scheduled the softball tryouts to begin the last Saturday in April. As Matt played catch with Ryan, loosening up his arm, he kept one eye on the street above the playing field, hoping to catch a glimpse of Ben. Maybe Ben would change his mind at the last minute.

"Look out!" Ryan shouted. He had let the ball fly while Matt's attention had been diverted.

Matt caught sight of the ball streaking toward his face. He shot up his gloved hand at the last second.

"Keep your eye on the ball," Ryan admonished. "Before I end up injuring you. We can't afford to lose any more good players." He shook his head. "He'd be here by now," he added, "if he were going to show. It's not like Ben to be late."

Coach Leahy had organized the ball field into several stations, each one designed to evaluate a specific skill — throwing, shagging flies, fielding grounders, batting, sprinting. The players rotated in groups from station to station. Matt liked the fielding drill the best. Players formed two lines approximately thirty metres apart. Coach leahy would hit or throw a ball down the middle. The first player on the left would try to catch the ball while the first player in the other line covered the play. Matt loved the challenge of diving and coming up with the unexpected catch, robbing the cover man of the chance to play the ball.

Someone with a clipboard stood nearby evaluating each player on a scale of one to ten. Coach Leahy carried one too, as he wandered from station to station. The clipboards made Matt a little nervous, but it was kind of exciting too.

All the kids from last year were there, except Ben.

Kate confirmed the bad news. "He's not coming," she said. "He's made up his mind. He's already gone to a couple of hardball workouts in the gym. The coach told him he'll have no problem making the team."

The night after the second tryout Coach Leahy phoned Matt. "You're on the team," he said. "You'll be missing the final tryout, but it's not a problem. You're definitely there. In fact, I'm expecting you to take a strong leadership role this year."

"Great," Matt responded enthusiastically. He paused for a moment.

Coach Leahy seemed to read his mind. "Your friends made it too. I've got everything pretty much figured out. Just a couple guys I need to decide on. I hope you all have a great time in Japan," he added.

"We will," Matt replied. "We will."

"And see if you can talk some sense into Ben while you're away. The Sharks still need to find a catcher."

* * *

Mrs. Bartley called the group together in the school library for one final meeting the week before their flight. "I hope you've all sent off your letters to your host family," she said.

Matt had sent his a few weeks ago.

Dear Mr. and Mrs. Ozaki:

Hi! My name is Matt. Matt Tucker to be exact.
I'm fourteen and in grade nine at Adam Scott High
School. There are four people in my family. You
can tell from the picture that Mom and I look alike.
Kevin, my older brother, looks a lot like my Dad.

I like sports, especially softball. I play for a
team called the East City Sharks. Are there sharks
in Japan? I hope so. I play basketball too. I like to
draw and cook too, and sometimes I like to play
the piano. Most of the time, though, I play because
my mother makes me.

We have a pretty big house with a large garden.
I will bring a picture of it with me. We have two
pets in our house, a cat named Minou and a lizard.
My mother is forty-four years old. Her hobbies are
gardening, reading and sports. Mrs. Bartley said to
let you know what we would like to eat for breakfast. I usually eat eggs or cereal but my mother said
to tell you not to fuss. She says we will eat whatever you usually eat.

We are looking forward to staying with your
family.

Sincerely,

Matt Tucker

The Tuckers had received information regarding their host
family as well.

Ms. Tucker and Matt will stay with —

Mrs. and Mr. Masako and Hiroshi Ozaki. Mrs. Ozaki is a teacher at Daiichi Elementary School. Mr. Ozaki teaches at Daiichi Middle School. They have a son (Yoshiyasu, 12). Mr. Ozaki's parents (Yoshiko and Susumu) also live with them.

"The ball game is a go," the principal cheerfully announced. "A few details need to be ironed out, but you'll definitely be playing. In fact, we'll have two teams. Mr. Mai, our grade five teacher, will coach grades four to six. Mr. Crowley, with help from our grade seven teacher, Mr. Hart, will look after the older team. In Japan, grades seven, eight and nine are considered junior high so it works beautifully that we included the graduating class that's now at Adam Scott. They'll be visiting and playing against Daiichi Middle School." She began passing copies of the finalized itinerary around the room.

"What's this festival thing?" Mr. Byrd inquired. "Ryan and I couldn't find anything about the Otabi Festival on the Internet. We found lots of other festivals, the Obon festival of lanterns, and the Children's Festival where they fly all those carp streamers and things. They seem to have festivals for just about everything. Unfortunately," he sighed heavily, "we couldn't find anything about this one."

Ryan leaned forward on his chair and poked Matt in the back with his pencil. "Did you know Japan has a Ball Throwing Festival?" he whispered. "The Internet calls it a struggle between two groups of youths to catch a sacred wooden ball. It's supposed to bring good luck to the winning team."

"Every city in Japan is known for a specific festival," Mrs. Bartley was saying. "You'll be in Komatsu for the children's Otabi Festival. They've also noted here that Komatsu is famous for its *kabuki*." She shrugged her shoulders. "I'm sure you'll discover what that's all about when you arrive. Any further questions?"

Matt's mom slowly raised her hand. The principal acknowledged her with a quick nod.

"We've been hearing rumours about the toilets in Japan." Mrs. Tucker's normally pale face flushed slightly. "Do you know anything about Japanese toilets?" She caught Matt's eye and winked. Matt himself had been too shy to ask.

Mrs. Bartley laughed. "I stayed in a pretty luxurious hotel with a Western-style toilet when I was there, and there was at least one Western-style toilet at the school. I had no problems."

Matt's sigh of relief was audible.

"But," the principal continued, "you'll be staying in actual homes for a few days. I'm not exactly sure what you'll find there." She smiled reassuringly. "You'll be up for whatever comes your way, I'm sure. I've got confidence in you all." Suddenly, she placed her hands on her hips and mimicked a frown. "I'm jealous!" she exclaimed. "I wish I was going with you. We didn't get to do all this when I visited last year."

Matt was glad Mrs. Bartley had confidence in them. He was still feeling a little tentative about living with strangers who might not even speak English. And what if the house was really small? He had heard that Japanese homes and hotels were tiny. Would they all be jammed in tightly together?

The rest of the evening was spent going over details of the gift-giving that would be taking place. A separate suitcase would be required to transport the gifts for the schools, principals, interpreters, local dignitaries, even the bus drivers. He and his mom had already packed T-shirts, ball caps, maple syrup, books and Peterborough Liftlock pins for their host family. Mrs. Tucker had read somewhere that it was a good idea to take a few special treats for the younger children. She planned to take Anne of Green Gables stickers, Canadian flag pins and chocolate loonies and twoonies.

"Don't worry if you feel a little overwhelmed by the gift-giving," Mrs. Bartley warned. "It's impossible to match the generosity of the Japanese."

"*Sayonara*," she cried as the group left the room later that evening. "*Sayonara!*"

6

Konnichiwa

The Canadian Delegation, as the Japanese had labelled them, met at six o'clock in the morning in the school parking lot. An airport limousine service had been booked to transport the entire group to Toronto. Despite the uneasiness he often felt around Kate and Ben, and his lack of sleep the night before, Matt's entire body tingled with anticipation. It was as if a hundred thousand little grasshoppers were jumping around inside him, just under the surface of his skin.

On board the plane, however, a sense of nervousness over-took him. Matt clutched the armrests as the plane taxied down the runway.

"Take a few deep breaths," his mom advised. "That should help."

Eventually Matt began to relax. He gazed out the small, oval window. The city of Toronto, the shoreline of Lake Ontario, even the backyard swimming pools all took on fresh interest from his new perspective. And it felt good to be waited on — juice, food, ear phones, extra blankets. There was even a colourful little magazine for kids about major league baseball. Matt tried filling in the answers to the quiz on the back page. He had to match the diamond lingo on the left with the proper definitions on the right.

1. Sweet Spot	A. Home plate
2. Tater	B. A player's legs
3. Wheels	C. An easy catch by a fielder
4. Can of corn	D. The best part of a bat
5. Dish	E. A home run

He had never heard of "can of corn" before, except the ones found in the kitchen, but he knew all the rest so figured that one out using the process of elimination. "Piece of cake," he told the others. "Piece of cake."

The first leg of the flight was around five hours. They were to touch down in Vancouver, stop over for an hour, then catch a ten-hour flight to Nagoya. Nagoya was located in the center of Honshu, the largest of approximately three thousand islands that make up the country of Japan.

"The islands of Japan are the projecting summits of a huge chain of mountains," Mrs. Bartley had read to them. "Volcanoes are common, with the sacred volcano Fuji being the highest mountain. There are about two hundred volcanoes," she had added, "but only fifty are still active."

The information regarding volcanoes had startled Matt at first, along with the fact that Japan experiences numerous earthquakes. But when he discovered that more than a hundred and twenty million people lived there, he figured it couldn't be that dangerous.

Matt ate a light breakfast on the plane, then watched a movie. Occasionally, he studied the landscape below — the blues and greys of Georgian Bay, the winding Red River and contrasting high-rises of the city of Winnipeg, the patchwork quiltlike prairie farmland. When snow-capped mountains began appearing beneath him, he knew they must be getting close to Vancouver.

Before long, they began descending through drift after drift of fluffy, white clouds. Matt braced himself for the landing, but the plane's wheels touched down with a smoothness that astonished Matt and several of the other passengers as well.

An American soldier they met tried to teach the boys a little Japanese while they waited in the Vancouver airport. He had been stationed all over the world and could speak several languages.

"You probably know *sayonara* means goodbye," he stated matter-of-factly, "just from watching television."

Ryan and Matt nodded.

"*Konnichiwa* means good afternoon. Con-each-ee-wa," he added, slowly sounding out the word.

"*Konnichiwa*," Matt repeated.

"*Konnichiwa*." Ryan bowed deeply as he spoke.

"*Arigato* means thank you," he said.

"*Arigato*," Matt repeated.

"How do you say 'you're welcome'?" Ryan asked.

The man laughed. "That one's a little more difficult, but I'm sure you boys can do it. *Do-itashimashite*." Once again, he slowly sounded out the word. "Do-ee-tash-ee-mash-it-tay."

Matt and Ryan repeated the word over and over again until they finally had it mastered. "*Do-itashimashite*."

It was fun learning some basic Japanese and it made the hour stopover seem to fly by.

"*Sayonara*," the man called as Matt's group departed through the appropriate gate.

"*Sayonara*," Matt and Ryan chorused.

"*Arigato*," added Matt.

* * *

Once on board, Matt moved forward to sit with the guys. Kate and Ben were just across the aisle, holding hands. He was not aware of the deep frown that furrowed his brow.

"Buckle up," the stewardess reminded them all as she moved swiftly down the aisle. She was wearing a crisp, clean blue outfit with a red scarf, and she smiled a lot. After quickly giving the safety demo, she inserted a movie into the VCR.

It was hilarious, about a guy who was afraid to get married. All kinds of crazy, humiliating things kept happening to him. Matt glanced at Ben out of the corner of his eye. He hoped Ben was watching. Suddenly, Matt began chuckling quietly to himself. He and Ben had once seen a recipe for shark-fin soup in the newspaper. He couldn't remember if it was Chinese or Japanese, but it was definitely Asian, and at the end of the recipe it had said that it was an aph ... an aphro ... disiac, aphrodisiac. Yes, that was it. Matt had never heard of the word but Ben knew what it meant.

"Some kind of love potion," he had said, dark eyes glittering playfully. "It's supposed to make you feel romantic. Chocolate does the same thing. Did you know that? That's why people always give it to each other on Valentine's Day."

Maybe in Japan, Matt figured, he could find some kind of recipe that would do just the opposite. He would serve Ben a gigantic portion. He let his mind wander as he pondered possible names that could appear on a menu — turtle-toe soup, eye of octopus ...

Matt started. The stewardess had placed trays of food in front of him and Ryan. "Is this what they call sushi?" he asked, pulling the dish close to his nose and sniffing. It smelled different than anything he had ever smelled before. He had liked the chicken they had served earlier, but this — this looked and smelled, well, Japanese. There were four little portions of rice. Two were rectangular with raw fish laid overtop. Two had been rolled around colourful little bits of things that Matt did not recognize. Flat, green stuff was wrapped around the sides of one.

"*Nori*," someone said. "Seaweed."

Matt grimaced. He was not about to eat seaweed. He glanced over at Ben's plate. He had already finished off his second one.

"They're good," Ben said.

When the stewardess finally removed Matt's untouched tray, he pulled his knapsack out of the compartment above and retrieved a couple packs of cheese snacks and a large bag of chips. Finally feeling full, he leaned back in his seat and closed his eyes.

Seconds later, it seemed, Ryan was poking him in the ribs. "Matt, Matt," he cried. "We're in Japan."

"We're in Japan." His friend spoke louder this time and jabbed again, hard. "You've been sleeping for hours. Some fun you turned out to be."

Matt's eyes opened reluctantly. "Japan?" he stammered groggily. "Japan?" Everything seemed hazy, fuzzy, as if he had awakened from a dream. He gazed out the window over the wing to the ground below. Rice field after rice field passed beneath him, then masses of elaborately tiled rooftops began to appear, seemingly overlapping each other.

He shook himself fully awake. It was no dream. They were really here! They were in Japan!

"*Konnichiwa*," Matt called out excitedly. "*Konnichiwa*."

7

Nagoya

Matt could see the airport in Nagoya was very different from Pearson International in Toronto. For one thing it was smaller. People didn't shove or bump into you as if you didn't matter. No little metal slots were waiting to swallow up your coins just so you could get a cart for your luggage. Everyone seemed friendlier, too — courteous, eager to please. And there was lots of bowing going on.

People were hustling about, mostly dressed in clothes similiar to what Matt saw in Canada. A lot of the men were wearing dark business suits while some of the teens, even the young kids, were clad in dark blue or black uniforms. And just like back in Canada, every once in a while a teenager with bright orange or green dyed hair would walk by. Matt had bleached his hair blonder a few times, but he had never tried anything quite that dramatic. His father would kill him if he ever came home looking like that.

Matt and his mom showed their joint passport to the friendly man behind the counter and then quickly wove their way behind the others, toward two Japanese women standing just beyond the customs gate. They were teachers from Daiichi and they were waving frantically in the direction of Mr. Mai and Mr. Hart, the teachers with the group who had been to Japan on exchange before.

Both women had short dark hair. One of them was tall; the other short. The shorter woman was wearing glasses and she had a sprinkling of freckles. Matt caught himself staring. He didn't know Japanese people had freckles.

"*Konnichiwa*," they called in unison. "*Konnichiwa*. Good afternoon and welcome to Japan."

"My name is Naigai," the tallest of the two announced cheerfully. "And this is Ria," she added, pointing to her friend. "How was your flight?"

"Some of you may wish to use the restroom," Ria quickly suggested as the group made its way toward the pickup area. "Before we load up the bus. We still have quite a drive ahead of us," she warned.

This is it, Matt told himself, glancing in Ben and Kate's direction. Did they remember their conversation that day back in the hall at Adam Scott, how they had speculated about the toilets in Japan?

But Ben was oblivious, to Matt, to the others, to what the two Japanese women were saying. He was bent over, busy helping Kate with her luggage.

Matt sighed and followed along, past souvenir shops and vending machines to the far end of the building. Just about anything you could think of was available in the vending machines, even beer and cigarettes.

Naigai and Ria directed them to two doorways with Japanese characters and little pictures of a man and a woman beneath.

Matt exhaled a sigh of relief as he entered the appropriate doorway. In many ways the Japanese washroom looked much like public washrooms at home. There were cubicles along one side of the room and urinals lined up along the opposite wall. They were a little smaller than those in North America, but very clean. Automatic flush, he noted. A large mirror hung on the wall over a few sinks, just like back at home.

The stall near the front of the washroom had a small rectangular sign posted on it. *WESTERN*, it read. Steve Hutton stepped through the door of the Western toilet. Ben Aoki swung open an unmarked door. The other boys crowded around.

8

Toilet Talk

The bus was crammed with luggage and people, but once on board, Matt stared out the window and marveled at the sights and sounds they encountered as they sped through the streets of Nagoya. "Look!" he shouted. "There's a ball diamond!"

"Hardball, I think," Mr. Crowley added.

"And over there," Mike said, pointing to the left. He spoke hesitantly. "I ... I think it's golf."

"A driving range," someone offered from the back. A large net had been strung across the sky as if giants were about to play a game of volleyball.

"It's amazing, how all the space is so well utilized," Mrs. Tucker remarked, clucking her approval. "Each house, no matter how small, has a lovely little garden."

Matt kept his eye out whenever they passed what he thought might be a factory, just in case there was one like the Barries had mentioned.

Suddenly a burst of laughter erupted in the middle of the bus. A discussion regarding Japanese toilets had broken out.

"Did you notice there were no paper towels in the washroom?" someone was saying. "I think people are supposed to carry something with them to dry their hands on."

Naigai nodded. "It keeps garbage to a minimum. You'll notice schools are like that too. Each student is expected to carry a little white handkerchief in their pocket."

"You may want to carry tissue with you as well," Ria advised. "Some of the more tradional toilets downtown do not always supply toilet paper."

"The toilet paper was non-perforated," Steve offered. "Did you guys pick up on that?"

Some of the younger kids looked puzzled.

"You know, none of the little indentations across the roll which make it easier to tear off," he explained.

"It's no wonder the Japanese people have a better work ethic than we do," Mr. Retallick added, laughing heartily. He had done quite a bit of reading beforehand in preparation for the trip with his sons Stephen and Shaun.

"Well, I'm really proud of myself," Anna Aoki stated. "I used the Japanese toilet. It scared me a bit at first," she confessed, beginning to giggle. "It looked like an upended urinal lying there, staring up at me, helpless, flat out on its back. I didn't know exactly what to do, but I gave it my best shot. Ria helped out a bit too. She said to face the end with the little raised hood."

"I just waited in line for the Western one," Mrs. Tucker admitted. Matt smiled to himself. So had he.

"I do like the idea of the heated seat," his mother added.

"You don't heat toilet seats in Canada?" Ria asked, dark brows and eyes raising increduously.

A chorus of loud "no's" arose from the passengers on the bus.

"But it is so cold over there," she added.

Kate waited patiently for the noise to die down. "Some of us do," she said, grinning impishly.

Matt flashed a bewildered look in her direction.

"At our family's cottage," Kate began, "on Lake Catchacoma. Whenever it got cold outside, my Uncle Dave would bring the toilet seat in to hang by the fireplace. Whoever went to the outhouse would take the seat out with them."

Naigai and Ria giggled simultaneously.

"We even have a picture of Aunt Sandi hanging by the fireplace, her head inside the seat."

Everyone was laughing now, including the bus driver who didn't even speak or understand English. His broad shoulders jostled jovially.

"Wait, wait," Kate continued. "Uncle Ken, who's always fooling around building stuff, hooked up this wire thingama-jig. Aunt Ruth was a little skeptical at first but now she loves it. Whenever the power in the cottage is turned on, the toilet seat heats up automatically." Kate flicked her long auburn hair off her shoulders. "Pretty cool, eh?"

Ria, still laughing, reached across the aisle and touched a loose strand of Kate's hair. Her eyes quickly panned the bus. "This is just one thing I love about you Canadians. You have such incredibly coloured hair." Looking admiringly into Kate's bright blue eyes, she continued, "I am going to call you *Akage no Kate*. You remind me of *Akage no An*, red-haired Anne, the famous Anne of P.E.I." She leaned forward, closer to Kate. "*Akage no Kate*, you tell your uncles to keep working on that toilet seat. Here in Japan many toilet seats are not only heated, they'll weigh you, check your blood pressure — some toilets even chemically analyse urine."

"Wow," Matt exclaimed. "That's, that's amazing."

* * *

The bus had left the city of Nagoya behind and was meandering through a scenic mountainous region. The tree-clad mountain-sides provided a perfect backdrop for hanging purple wisteria, orange honeysuckle and light green maples. Wispy white clouds hovered on the tops of the mountains like lingering puffs of smoke.

Periodically, the bus made its way through dark narrow tunnels carved straight through the rock. Small cemeteries

seemed to be everywhere, sometimes teetering precariously
on narrow mountain ridges, sometimes standing stark in the
middle of a rice field.

Nestled at the base of each and every mountain was rice
field after rice field, army after army of little green shoots all
standing at attention. Occasionally an older person, head covered, could be seen in the fields working diligently.

And every once in a while, much to Matt's delight, a ball
diamond seemed to pop up, almost out of nowhere. "The
Japanese people must love baseball," Matt exclaimed.

"*Besuboru*, we call it," Naigai said, smiling, pleased her
visitors were enjoying themselves. "And you are exactly right.
We do love it. Baseball is Japan's leading spectator sport."

"How come?" Ben asked.

"Although we borrowed the game from the West," Naigai
admitted, "some say we Japanese fully appreciate it because it
is a game with order and harmony."

"Some people say hardball is too slow," Ben continued,
glancing briefly in Matt's direction. "But these are all hardball diamonds. Why hardball?"

"Perhaps that is why we love it," Naigai suggested. "The
slowness of the game allows the spectator to pay attention to
its every detail. You will notice while you are here that we
Japanese are very appreciative of detail."

"We like the drama of the game as well," Ria said. "Especially the duels between the pitcher and batter. And there is
tremendous concentration required to play ball. Is there not?"

Ben nodded.

"Just as concentration is required during meditation," Ria
added. "It is a good game for us Japanese." She opened a large
bag of cellophane-wrapped buns, and began passing them
back to everyone on the bus.

They were incredibly tasty, Matt decided, after polishing
off his second one. The first had been full of melted butter, the

second held a delicious fruit centre. It appeared he was not going to starve to death after all.

As Matt sat in his hotel room later that evening, a contented feeling swept over him. The rice fields beyond his window glowed with the reflected light of sunset. He could almost feel the warmth of the oranges and yellows, the purplish pinks. It was the first time he had felt this happy since he and Ben had stopped being best friends. He was sipping tea, wearing the crisp, clean kimono-like *yukata* and white slippers that had been laid out on the bed. The toilet was Western style. He had noticed that right off. One thing puzzled him though — the little digital control panel at the side of it, lit up like the cockpit of an airplane. He would have to ask someone about that later. Bath beads, soap, even a small travel-sized toothbrush and mini-pack of toothpaste had all been provided, arranged neatly on the countertop.

Everything about the Hotel Plaza Lyon was luxurious — the lobby, the restaurant, the rooms themselves. His mother was soaking in the oversized tub that very minute.

Matt studied his tea cup as he rotated it slowly in his hands. It was shiny, turquoise blue with a picture of what appeared to be two cranes ... dancing? The cranes were white with splashes of black here and there and a small patch of red on top of their heads.

Naigai had been right about details. There had even been a small, glass fish-shaped thing that matched the teacup. You were supposed to set the used teabag on it, his mother had told him. Japan was definitely going to be okay, Matt decided. In fact, it would be better than that. Like Mrs. Bartley had said, it was going to be the experience of a lifetime. He shivered, like he sometimes did at church when someone with a really great voice hit and held a high note. A country this awesome, he figured, with the same passion for ball that he had, was going to be pretty amazing.

9

The Ozakis

The chirp, chirp, chirping of birds woke Matt early the next morning. In actual fact, it was a tape of birds chirping, being played in the hallways of the hotel at six o'clock. Despite his tiredness, Matt had awakened several times during the night.

"It's a good thing we're not playing ball today." Matt yawned and stretched as he spoke. "I'm still really tired. I hardly slept at all."

"Your system needs to adjust," his mom said, red-eyed and weary, grasping for words in the midst of an enormous yawn. "Last night ... it was ... daytime back home ... your body knows it. It'll take a few days."

"How many?" Matt asked, voice carrying an edge of alarm. "We want to be in top shape for the game."

"Two, probably three at most."

"Phew!" Matt wiped his brow with the back of his hand. "It's a good thing we're not playing until the end of the week."

* * *

A welcome brunch was held at the hotel in honour of the Canadian delegation. Speeches were delivered, songs sung, introductions made, gifts presented. And again, there was lots of bowing.

Matt found it hard to concentrate on formalities. His eyes perused the tables. He was really hungry, but it was how it all looked that surprised him. He had never seen food displayed quite so wonderfully before — trays laden with fruits and vegetables, salads, fancy sandwiches, spaghetti, meatballs, several different types of shrimp and chicken. There were even french fries. And then dessert — little cheesecakes, dark and white chocolate, more fruit and special little cookies. Everything looked fresh and colourful, and they had done really amazing things, like arranging the little cherry tomatoes in patterns and carving the carrots into cranes. He definitely wasn't going to starve to death.

Then again, maybe he would, if he had to use the chopsticks he was handed. Everything kept falling off. Finally, the vice-principal of Daiichi Elementary offered a quick lesson.

"First chopstick, hold still, against thumb," he instructed, demonstrating as he spoke. He was a medium-sized man, with extremely thick dark hair and a boyish grin. "Hold close to end like pencil," he added. "Second chopstick move to pick up food. Like this." The man quickly flipped his chopsticks over as he reached for more salad from the bowl on the table. "Pick food from table with chopsticks upside down. Use end, not been in mouth."

It was pretty slow going but Matt managed. In fact, it was kind of fun. Only problem was, you couldn't wolf down the food the way he and the guys did at home. That should make his mother happy. She was always complaining about that.

After the meal, a Japanese man demonstrated the *kendama*, a traditional wooden toy. The wooden part looked like a hammer. It had a small, red ball attached to it by a long piece of string. The man held the wooden part at almost arm's length and jerked the ball upward. There were four spots on the toy where you could catch the ball. He was good at it, but he could not get the ball to land on the pointy end.

He handed his *kendama* over to Matt, then passed out several more. Matt tried again and again. It was harder than it looked. Suddenly, a loud cheer erupted. Matt looked up. Ben had successfully landed his ball.

Matt set his jaw determinedly and pursed his lips. "Finally," he muttered a minute later, smiling proudly as the shiny applelike sphere landed snugly in its wooden cradle.

"You ... keep," the man said, bowing deeply, friendly eyes twinkling, as he presented Matt with the *kendama*.

The Tuckers left the hotel that afternoon with Mr. and Mrs. Ozaki. Mrs. Ozaki was taller than her husband, quite a bit taller than Matt and his mom. Naigai was tall too, Matt remembered. He had been surprised when he first saw her, because he had thought all Japanese people were short. Mr. Ozaki had greying black hair, a round face and glasses. He looked very businesslike in his dark jacket and dress pants.

Matt's host family lived in a nearby village about twenty minutes from Komatsu. The streets were narrow and crowded, but the cars and trucks were small and the traffic seemed to flow with a courteous give and take that was remarkable.

The Ozakis' house did not look large from the outside, where several bonsai pine trees were lined up in pots. Hedges of pink azaleas flanked the cement driveway. A Japanese maple that matched the dark red of the tiled roof, yellow iris and peony all dotted the moss-covered rockery. Two *bonsai* purple wisteria framed the doorstep.

The house wasn't square or rectangular like most Canadian homes. It seemed to jut out here and there, with different parts of the house being made of wood, metal and other materials. There was something that looked like the frame of a greenhouse in front of one part, as well as a funny-looking contraption that held laundry. A rice field was located right behind the house.

Immediately upon entering, Matt reached in his sack for his slippers. Mrs. Tucker did the same.

Mr. Ozaki gestured toward their feet. "*I-ye, i-ye,*" he said. "No, No."

"No slippers," Mrs. Ozaki added.

"Yes, yes," Mrs. Tucker insisted. "We will wear our slippers. It is good manners," she whispered to Matt, "to wear slippers in a Japanese home."

Mr. Ozaki immediately turned their shoes around so the toes faced the doorway.

"Custom," his wife explained. "Many homes influence by West," she added. "Ours, traditional Japanese. Sit ... floor ... most time." She pointed to the brightly coloured pillows on the floor. "*Tatami* mats," she explained, directing their attention to the strawlike woven material covering the floor on the flat area above the foyer.

"It not only looks good," Matt's mom said, inhaling the sweet grassy aroma. "It smells good too." She bent down and ran one hand over the smooth, woven surface.

"Rice straw," Mrs. Ozaki said. "Follow," she beckoned, smiling pleasantly. "Please."

Inside, the house was incredibly spacious, much larger than Matt had expected. Most floors were covered in *tatami*. Beautiful sliding paper screens separated the rooms. One had a mountain scene on it, another a view of the sea. A small pit occupied the centre of the main living room.

Mrs. Ozaki noticed Matt's puzzled expression. "A *ko-tatsu*," she explained.

Both Matt and his mom still looked perplexed.

"Ah!" Mrs. Ozaki cried. Her eyes, like fireflies, ignited suddenly. "You know hibachi?" she queried.

Her visitors nodded.

.bachi." She paused for a brief
ɔper English words. "Heat house,

the *kotatsu*. Perched on an upper
was a TV. Matt smiled. He knew
other furniture in the room.
ɪ... ɹed the Ozakis through another sliding
doorway.

"Altars, this rᴏ m," Mrs. Ozaki explained. "In Shinto," she said directing their gaze to the corner of the room, "we honour ancestors. A colourful doll, a vase of flowers and two wooden statues were all arranged neatly on a raised wooden alcove. "Many gods in nature, too — sun, moon, rocks, wind. Buddha behind wall," she added. "In August we celebrate Obon, festival of lanterns, offer food to ancestors — rice, vegetables, fruit. Japanese people, Shintoist and Buddhist. Have many, many gods.

"Call me Masako," Mrs. Ozaki instructed warmly, as she led them into the adjoining room where thick bedding materials were stacked neatly in one corner. A couple of pillows topped the pile. "Sleep on floor, futons," Masako said. "*Makuro*," she added, handing a pillow to Matt. "Pillows of rice."

"*Makuro*," Matt repeated, carefully turning the small pillow in his hands. "Wow," he exclaimed, catching his mother's eye. "The pillows really are made of rice."

"Very, very comfortable," Masako added.

Her husband nodded. "Hai, hai."

"You will need bathroom, sometimes," their hostess chuckled. "Maybe soon. I show now." She beckoned them to follow.

Matt's mind raced. It would probably be a traditonal Japanese-style toilet, he figured. The bed was. The rest of the house seemed to be. Of course, it would be too. He braced himself as he entered the doorway. He did not want to appear rude.

"Put on, to use toilet," Masako instructed, drawing their attention to three pairs of garishly pink plastic slippers that were parked by the door. "Forget to take off, see pink, soon remember."

Matt's face broke into a broad smile. Sure, the slippers were kind of funny looking, but what had really made him smile were the toilets themselves. There were two little cubicles inside the bathroom, one labelled "Western style" by a sign hanging right on its door. Masako pushed the door open. It was almost the same toilet as the one at the hotel. He'd bet the seat was heated. That's what the panel had been for, to control the temperature of the seat. The other cubicle contained a traditonal Japanese toilet. There was also a small sink in the corner, but there was no tub or shower.

"Bath, wash, other part of house," Masako continued, "beside kitchen."

The four of them made their way back through the living room. The bathing area was in two separate rooms. One had a large mirror, a huge sink and cupboards. The other room held the tub and shower. The tub was deep and full of hot water. A little blue plastic stool stood nearby with a portable shower head above it.

"Japanese people," Masako began, "wash first, before bath."

* * *

The entire family gathered in the kitchen for dinner that evening. It was not as large as the other rooms, but it seemed to have everything — fridge, stove, sink, cupboards. It was the only room with a Western-style table and chairs.

Mr. Ozaki introduced his son to the Tuckers. "Yoshiyasu," he said, gesturing toward his son.

Yoshiyasu bowed deeply.

"You say, Yoshi," Mrs. Ozaki advised. "Easier."

"My name is Matt," Matt replied, returning the gesture.

"Matt," Yoshi repeated. "Matt."

Matt studied the twelve-year-old boy. He was quite a bit shorter than Matt, with dark brown hair and friendly brown eyes. He was wearing blue jeans and a T-shirt, and he had put his slippers on as he entered the kitchen. He would fit right in back at home, Matt thought. In fact, in many ways he reminded him of Ben.

"Grade eight, Daiichi Middle School," Masako informed.

Yoshi grinned shyly at Matt and his mother.

"Husband, Hiroshi. He teach there." She tapped herself in the chest. "I teach, ele ... mentary, grade six."

The parents of Mr. Ozaki lived in a separate part of the same house. Mr. Ozaki senior had been working in his nearby farm plot most of the day. His wife had been busy preparing dinner. They were both short, both wore glasses and both had that same engaging sparkle in their dark brown eyes.

That night Matt tasted many foods he had never heard of — devil fish and squid, bamboo baby, a special kind of pork cooked inside a crispy coating and rice. The rice was sticky, not fluffy and dry like the rice back home. It was a good thing, Matt decided. How could you eat fluffy rice with chopsticks? The Ozakis laughed a lot during the meal at the Tuckers' efforts to use the chopsticks and at the expressions on their faces as they tasted the different foods.

Again, a wonderful feeling of contentment swept over Matt. A lot of the food was really tasty. This Yoshi kid was all right. And it was amazing how much fun they were having, even though many of them could not fully communicate. A constant flurry of hand gestures had accompanied the meal, as if they were playing a game of charades. Occasionally, Masako and Hiroshi would consult a small hand-held computerized interpreter. Matt or his mom would type in an English word and instantly the Japanese equivalent would appear on the small screen.

"*Hai, hai*," they would cry.

Matt found himself wondering about Ben's host family. Were they traditional Japanese? What was Ben eating for supper? For a few seconds he'd competely forgotten that he and Ben were barely talking.

After dinner Matt and Yoshi practised using the *kendama*. Yoshi brought out a spinning toy called a *komo*, then showed Matt his baseball glove. It was well worn and seemed expensive. For some reason Matt had expected the gloves to be inferior to the ones in Canada. Yoshi, Matt suddenly realized, would probably be playing against him.

The grandmother showed Matt how to make a couple of *origami* animals with small squares of coloured paper. First they made a rabbit, then a crane.

"In ancient Japan," Yoshi slowly explained, "paper have spirit … fold, no cut, keep spirit alive."

Matt looked up at Yoshi, surprised to hear him speak English so well. He had just been a little shy at dinner, Matt realized. They would be able to communicate after all.

Later that evening Matt's mother was presented with two beautifully handcrafted *temari* balls. One had a multicoloured star design; the other was yellow and red with a small green frog worked onto the surface.

"Traditional girl's toy," Masako elaborated. "Now, craft. Husband's mother make."

"They're exquisite," Mrs Tucker exclaimed, turning them carefully in her hands.

The Japanese people sure love balls, Matt wrote in his journal later that evening, after they had prepared their futons for bedtime. *There are balls and ball diamonds everywhere.* As he began to doodle in the margins of his journal a *kendama* took shape, then a *temari* ball. Suddenly, from his mother's futon there came a loud gasp.

10

Ohayo

Mrs. Tucker had been lying on her futon reading *Frommer's Guide to Japan*. She started to read aloud:

> Nothing is so distastful to the Japanese as the bottoms of shoes. Therefore, you should take off your shoes before entering a home, a Japanese-style inn, a temple, and even some museums or restaurants. Usually, there will be some plastic slippers at the entranceway for you to slip on, but whenever you encounter *tatami*, you should take off even your slippers — only bare feet or socks are allowed to tread upon *tatami*.

"We are not supposed to wear our slippers in this home," Marg Tucker cried. "Only in the kitchen or the toilet area. The rest of the house is *tatami*. I feel like such a fool. I should have read up on this before we came, but I just didn't have the time. We must apologize to the Ozakis first thing in the morning."

Mrs. Tucker emerged from the bedroom early the next day, guide book in hand, clean white socks on her feet.

"Good morning." Masako waved cheerfully from the kitchen. "*Ohayo gozaimasu.*"

Matt's mom approached the doorway. "*Ohayo gozaimasu,*" she replied. She pointed to the passage in the book, her feet, then the *tatami* mat below. "It says here, no slippers on *tatami* mats. I'm sorry, I did not know."

Masako nodded, her narrow, fine features crinkling with laughter. She began speaking in rapid Japanese, sharing with the others gathered around the table what had happened. Laughter filled the room.

Matt stumbled groggily into the living room to see what all the fuss was about.

"Yes," Masako was saying. "Sock feet, *tatami*; slippers, kitchen." She bent over and picked up the little wooden stand that was near the doorway of the two adjoining rooms. "Keep slippers, here."

Matt rubbed the sleep from his eyes as he ran everything through his mind. He was to wear his socks in most of the house, the ugly pink things in the bathroom and finally, his own slippers when he came into the kitchen. How would he ever remember it all? Japan sounded complicated.

Dressing in a kimono was complicated too, he decided, as he watched Yoshi's grandmother outfit his mother later that morning.

"We wear these on special occasions," Masako said. "Today, go to town, Komatsu Otabi Festival."

Dozens of dragonflies darted and danced about on the surface of the pale pink fabric. A brilliant burgandy *obi* sash was wrapped around Mrs. Tucker's waist and tied in back with a butterfly knot.

Masako continued, while the grandmother worked. "Long ago festival show gratitude to castle lord. People travel street to street. That is why called Otabi. Now celebrate with food, games, music, drama."

Matt laughed when he saw the *tabi*, or kimono socks. Three of his mom's toes fit in one part of each tight white sock, two in the other part. He had a vague feeling he had seen something like this before. Finally, it hit him. It was the calf his friend Sheldon, from hockey, had shown at the Peterborough Exhibition — it had split hooves. Matt kept his thoughts to himself. He was sure his mother would not appreciate hearing the fact that she reminded him of a cow.

There were several women dressed in kimonos at the festival. Some of them were walking on tall wooden clogs and had heavily painted faces. A group of boys Matt's age were manoeuvering about under an elaborate dragon costume.

"Dragon dance," Yoshi explained. "Invented to drive away sickness and disease, now folk dance for festivals, special occasions."

Matt and Yoshi were joined by Ryan and his Japanese host, Kazuki. They wandered through the food and game booths. Again, Matt thought of the Peterborough Ex. There were games of skill and chance similar to the ones back home. The fish pond here was a little more exciting, though — you could catch real live *koi* carp to exchange for prizes. Matt and Ryan had a lot of fun competing with Yoshi and Kazuki.

Matt noticed that Yoshi had a deadly accurate throwing arm. "Do you play ball on your school team?" he asked.

"*Besuboru?*" Yoshi queried.

"Yes, yes," Matt cried. "Do you play?"

"*Hai, hai,*" Yoshi replied. He pointed to Kazuki. "He play too."

The highlight of the festival was the children's *kabuki*. The entire Canadian delegation gathered to watch this unique form of theatre. The costumes were gorgeous and the plays were performed on elaborate movable *hikiyama* stages that were carried around the city. Matt had a difficult time figuring out what was going on. The program said it was a play about loyalty and selflessness. He quickly glanced in Ben's direction. For a brief moment, their eyes locked. Matt hoped he had noticed the same little blurb. Loyalty and the importance of the team was supposed to be a big Japanese thing, wasn't it?

Maybe Ben would take the hint and come back to the East City Sharks.

More importantly, Matt realized, he wanted Ben back as a friend; he wanted that more than he cared to admit. Sure, Ryan and the rest of the guys were a lot of fun, but it just wasn't the same. Even though he and Ben were different in many ways, they had many similarites as well. They were both competitive and were pretty evenly matched physically. Whether it was one-on-one with a basketball, a game of skunk with a softball and glove or a race in a pool, it was always exciting. You never knew who would win from one day to the next.

And he could talk to Ben about anything. If he was in trouble at home or at school Ben was always the first to know. It had worked both ways — at least until now. Ever since grade one Matt had been the one Ben had confided in. But now, Ben was always with Kate.

* * *

A traditional Japanese dinner was provided by the local men's cooking club that evening. Traditional Japanese, Matt soon realized, meant you sat on pillows on the floor. Again, the amount as well as the beauty of the food astounded him. The adults raved about the *tempura* — small bits of fish and vegetables covered in a fluffy, yet crispy, melt-in-your-mouth coating. Matt's favourite turned out to be the gross-looking black spaghetti. He had been afraid to try it at first, but one of the cooks, the one with the incredible sense of humour, wouldn't take no for an answer.

"*Ikasumi* spaghetti," the man said. "Different?"

Matt nodded.

"Be courageous. Very good."

Matt started with a small portion, but ended up asking for more — three times!

Yoshi couldn't stop laughing as he watched his new-found friend eat.

"Sauce, black ink from cuttlefish," the man explained.

* * *

Back at the Ozakis' Matt played catch with Yoshi in the street in front of the house. His instincts had been correct. Yoshi was a good player, a great player in fact, but Matt was most impressed by the accuracy of his arm.

"I catcher," Yoshi explained. "On school team."

His father, who was standing nearby, smiled proudly.

That explains it, Matt thought. A catcher would need to be deadly accurate. Matt needed to be, as well, because houses, cars, flower beds, even rice fields were all dangerously close.

Before bed Matt made another entry in his journal.

> *Japan is very different from Canada. Here, it is polite to slurp when you eat noodles and to drink soup out of the bowl. You never take soap into the tub. People wash first before they bathe. They often bathe together in spas or communal bathhouses. It's kind of like a social event. The biggest difference though, is the fact that you have to think about your feet a lot so you don't make a mistake like we did the first night.*
>
> *Yoshi, my host, is pretty cool. He's a great ball player, a catcher, like Ben. Today, we went to the Otabi Festival. It was fun playing the games with Yoshi and Kazuki, Ryan's host. I liked the dragon dance the best.*

Again, Matt began to sketch. He had always enjoyed draw-ing, but something seemed different this time. He felt like putting more effort into it, adding more details, trying to capture the feeling of motion ...

11

Sunny Side Up

For the first time since coming to Japan, Matt slept soundly. It was the third day of their stay; his mother had been right. Why was he always surprised when that happened?

"Finally," Matt announced, quickly grabbing his slippers upon bouncing into the kitchen, "I've got lots of energy." He turned and addressed his mom. "I bet I could play ball today."

"You won't be playing for a while yet," Mrs. Tucker said. "The game at the middle school is still three days away."

Masako spoke quickly with her husband. Hiroshi looked in Matt's direction, smiled and nodded.

What's going on? Matt wondered.

"You good player," Masako said. "Husband coach baseball, Yoshi's team, middle school. We go after school one day. You practise with team, with Yoshi."

Matt's face broke into a broad grin. This was unbelievable. He was actually living with the coach of the opposition. "*Hai, hai,*" he agreed excitedly. He turned and gave Yoshi a high-five. It was perfect. Not only would he get a chance to brush up on his skills before the challenge game, he would have an opportunity to scout out the opposition.

Most of the Ozakis ate rice and squid for breakfast. A little tough compared to shark, but not bad, Matt decided. There was also cereal on the table, tiny croissants and milk — not 1% or 2%, but 3.7%.

As Masako pulled a small carton of eggs out of the refrigerator, Matt spoke up. "I'm good at cooking eggs," he said. "Would you like me to cook one for you?"

"Yes, yes," she replied.

"What kind?" Matt asked. "Sunny side up? Over easy?"

"What, sunny side?" Masako asked.

Matt cracked open a shell and poured the egg into the hot pan. He pointed to the bright orange yolk. "Sunny side," he explained. "That's how I like mine."

Masako's head tilted back as she laughed. She passed the information on to the others. "We say, eye big," she said, turning to face Matt once again.

It was Matt's turn to laugh. It was amazing how the same things could be seen so differently.

"People say," Masako began, "Japan, land of rising sun. Japan mean source of sun. Shinto sun goddess, most famous. Sun important to Japanese." She laughed again. "I say sunny side up."

12

Sharks, Shrines and Samurai

A flurry of sightseeing consumed the Canadian delegation the next day. Naigai and Ria accompanied the group, along with several men from the local Parent Teacher Association.

"First stop, Sea of Japan," Ria announced.

"Are there any sharks in the sea?" Matt asked.

"Not here," Ria replied, shaking her head reassuringly.

She creased her brow, bewildered, when she noticed Matt's face drop in disappointment. "Island of Okinawa, many, many sharks," she quickly added.

"Japan home to some of the rarest of sharks," Naigai offered when she realized Matt's interest. "Very rare dwarf shark off shores of Japan, only six inches long."

"We also have goblin sharks," Ria said. "Do you know the goblin shark?"

"*Hai*." Matt nodded. The goblin was one of the most bizarre looking sharks of all, with a long, flat, pointy snout and oversized tail fin.

Shinto shrines, Buddhist temples and beautiful gardens were also on the day's agenda.

"Shinto shrines are the dwelling places of the gods," Naigai explained. "They are places of beauty too, so worshippers feel close to nature. Nature enhances feelings of peace and harmony."

There was a large basin with several ladles just inside the *torii*, the tall, red, wooden entrance to the shrine.

"We wash our hands before entering sacred grounds," Naigai explained. "This shows respect to the gods. That is why purification and cleanliness important to Japanese."

"We pull the rope to sound the gong and clap our hands to get the attention of the gods," Ria stated.

Matt was deep in thought. Why would you need to get the attention of the gods? Wouldn't a god already know everything?

"You ask favours of the gods," Ria added, tossing a coin. "Some shrines good for illness, or pregnancy." She tilted her head back as she began to laugh. "Others lucky for love."

Matt couldn't help but look in Ben and Kate's direction. He hoped this wasn't one of those. But he could see that it made sense, the fact that Ben was the first of the guys to have a girlfriend. He had always been more interested in girls than most of the others.

"Are there any that are good for baseball?" Ryan blurted.

"You get your fortunes here," Ria said, pulling Ryan close to the rows of bamboo sticks. "You pick out your fortune according to the number on your stick. If you like the fortune you take it home. If it is *kyo*, bad luck, simply tie your misfortune to the tree."

So that explains it. Matt had wondered why so many of the shrubs were covered in little white scraps of paper, fluttering about like blossoms waving in the wind.

* * *

The bus travelled on to the city of Kanizawa, where remains of an ancient castle stood near the entrance to Kenrokuen garden. Initially, Matt had not been thrilled about the idea of touring a garden. It had sounded like a boring thing to do. He soon changed his mind. Ponds, winding streams with stone bridges and waterfalls were all in abundance, filled with carp and turtles. Kate even spotted a water snake.

"Many things in Japan have meaning," Ria stated. "Carp are seen as symbols of strength, courage and patience."

"Back in Peterborough," Ryan offered, "carp are garbage-sucking giant fish that beg for food in that floor grate at the Riverview Park and Zoo."

"Next stop," Ria announced, "the Ninja Temple."

The temple was officially named the Miyoriyuji, but it had been nicknamed the Ninja-dera because of the hidden staircases, secret passageways and treacherous traps included in its architecture. They had been installed back in the time of the shoguns and samurai to outfox spies and enemies and to allow for sudden escapes. Matt and the others marveled at the ingenuity. Even the offertory box embedded in the floor near the main temple area was a trap.

The bottom of the temple was connected to a tunnel which led to Kanizawa Castle.

"Well water was used to make tea," their tour guide explained. "The ritual of the tea ceremony was important to samurai warriors — inspiration before battle, relaxation afterwards. A samurai warrior wore a distinctive headdress and magnificent protective armour," she added, pointing to the winged helmet in the nearby display case. "This identified him with the family he served."

Kind of like a team uniform, Matt thought. He could not imagine himself or Ben in anything but the red, white and black of the East City Sharks. He quickly drew a picture of the helmet in his mind so he could reconstruct it later in his journal. He paid careful attention to even the smallest detail.

"This is the way to the *seppuku* ritual suicide chamber," the guide continued as they climbed the uppermost staircase. "A samurai's loyalty was unconditional. They preferred to kill themselves rather than be captured by the enemy."

"The cherry blossom has come to symbolize loyalty," Naigai said. "It is also symbol of the samurai."

The students and parents in the group were all standing silent, mesmerized by the intrigue, mystery and history of the place. Matt's thoughts kept wandering back to Ben and the team. Did Ben not see it, the code of loyalty these samurai had? Being a samurai was like being part of a team. Loyalty was to be desired above all else. Ben was half-Japanese, so out of all the players on the Sharks, Matt figured he was the one that should know better.

As Matt climbed back on the bus, he couldn't help but wonder what the next day would bring. Each day was becoming more incredible than the one before. How could Peterborough have possibly compared with any of this?

Ben had been thinking the same thing. "Plain old Peterborough must have seemed pretty boring when you visited last summer," he said to the two Japanese teachers who were acting as interpreters.

"Oh, no," Naigai responded. "Although Japan is special and very rich in history and tradition, Peterborough is too, in its own way."

"Not like this," Ben added, waving his arms to emphasize his point.

"But you have so much green space and parks, and the houses have such large lawns and swimming pools, even." Her face flushed excitedly as she recalled the details of her trip. "And there are lots of lakes. We have lakes too, but many of your lakes and rivers are joined together. You can travel for many, many days by water."

"And the Lift Locks," Ria added, turning to face Naigai. "Remember, the magnificent Lift Locks? How the boats go up and down in two big bath tubs?" Her face grew thoughtful. "There is much to be gained from experiencing something different."

Naigai nodded in agreement. "In the next couple of days you will see how our schools are different."

Yes, thought Matt, he was looking forward to that. And he would get to go to Yoshi's ball practice. Would that be different too?

13

Daiichi

The entire group was scheduled to spend the next day at Daiichi Elementary. Matt and his mom rode to school with Masako Ozaki. Yoshi and his dad had already left for middle school, where the older kids would be visiting and playing ball the following day.

Matt packed his glove and sweats in his sports bag. He would be practising with Yoshi's team, the opposition, that very day.

Matt stared out the window of the small, silver Toyota as it snaked its way through the village back to the main road. The narrow streets were teeming with students, most in uniforms, most on bikes, all wearing large backpacks. Once in Komatsu they encountered hundreds of students on foot. To make crossing the streets safer, young children carried small yellow and black flags. Occasionally, Matt spotted someone wearing a white surgical mask, like the ones you'd see on a medical show on TV. "Why do they wear those?" he asked.

"Probably has cold," Masako explained. "Mask stop germs."

Nearer to Daiichi, Matt noticed that many of the students were wearing regular clothing.

"No uniforms at my school," Masako said as she turned into the small parking lot at the side of the building. Although it was the middle of the city, several irrigated rice fields glistened in the sun directly across the road from the school.

Daiichi Elementary was much larger than Queen Elizabeth Public School. Approximately six hundred students attended the large, beige three-storey facility. A shallow *koi* pond with a stone bridge and mossy rock garden lay nestled amongst several small pines to the right of the main entrance. The rest of the yard, including the ball diamond, was covered in light-coloured sand.

Two students stood propping open the doors for the others. "*Ohayo*," they cried loudly.

"*Ohayo*," their classmates responded. There was an edge of excitement and anticipation in the air.

Matt removed his shoes and shoved them into one of the small visitors' cubicles just inside the door. Mrs. Bartley had been right — a large room full of small cubbyholes was located nearby. Many students were gathered there, removing their shoes, chattering. The opposite wall featured a long, low row of sinks with mesh bags filled with bars of soap hanging from the faucets.

A welcome assembly was held in the gym, in honour of the Canadian delegation. The gym was as large as one at a Canadian high school. Two large bulletin boards formed a backdrop on the stage. One was covered with a Canadian flag and decorated with maple leaves; the other displayed a map of Japan, bedecked with pale pink cherry blossoms.

"Hey, that's the sun," Matt muttered, to no one in particular, when he saw the large red ball in the centre of the Japanese flag. He had never made the connection before.

Drum demonstrations, skits and songs were presented, all with an incredible degree of professionalism. The students had obviously practised a lot.

The classrooms proved similar to Canadian classrooms, except some seemed noisier. Matt was surprised. He had heard that the Japanese were shy and quiet. But, one thing was definitely different from back home — the noise halted abruptly as soon as the teacher addressed the class.

Daiichi had many features Matt had not expected to find in an elementary school — an infirmary, a large kitchen with five cooks, a broadcasting room …

"You will notice that each classroom has its own motto," Ria explained. She and Naigai had accompanied the group on the school tour. She pointed to four large carrots drawn on the wall at the back of the class and interpreted the Japanese characters written within.

We will be shining, happy and cheerful like the sun.
We will be challenging and strong like a storm.
We will be couragous and brave like a lion.
We will value each other's opinions.

The next room's motto was also translated.

We will cheerfully greet one another.
We will have our own opinions.
We will cooperate and help.
We will cherish our friends.

Matt felt his face flush as Ria finished reading the last sentence. Everything she had said was the exact opposite of the way he had been acting lately. He kept his head lowered, afraid the others might notice his embarrassment.

"It is time to stop for lunch," Naigai announced.

Good, thought Matt. He was hungry. Besides, he didn't want anyone to notice that this motto stuff was getting to him.

The group split up, a few of the Canadians joining each of several classrooms. Two students from each class had already hustled off to the kitchen where they had washed their hands and donned chef's hats and matching white coats. Each pair pushed a well-laden trolly up the elevator and back to their classroom where they served lunch to the others. Everyone bowed to each other before they began the meal, a tasty menu of salad, a special type of spaghetti, milk and jello. Matt decided he liked the Japanese system much better than packing and carrying his own lunch.

The most amazing thing happened next. Before proceeding to the playground, each and every student performed an assigned task. For the next fifteen minutes, the school hummed with the productive energy of a colony of busy worker ants. Girls, in groups of three, whisked small white mats down the hallways in front of their classrooms. A group of boys grabbed buckets and ran off to weed the small garden at the side of the schoolyard. A few others began sweeping the ground by the front entrance with large brooms. Every single student seemed to have a job to do.

"I hope the Canadian teachers don't get any ideas," Ryan blurted.

Matt and Steve nodded in agreement.

After the hustle and bustle subsided, the boys joined a group of grade six students out on the playground for a brief game of soccer. A few of the younger students were playing catch by the backstop. Others rode unicyles, played on the jungle gyms or slides. There were no adults in sight. While outside, Matt discovered later, the Daiichi students monitored themselves.

* * *

That afternoon the delegation took part in a calligraphy class, followed by a tea ceremony. Matt learned how to write his name in *katakana*, an alphabet of syllables used to write foreign words in Japanese.

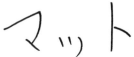

He had to duck upon entering the special room set apart for the tea ceremony. "The doorway is designed to make one bow upon entering," Naigai informed, "to encourage humility of character. The tea house is most often set in a garden but we have re-created one here. We want the students to experience the richness of their traditions and culture."

Two Japanese students dressed in kimonos made the tea. They poured hot water into a green powder, then stirred the mixture with a bamboo whisk. The whole process seemed slow and kind of boring, Matt decided, but he did his best to kneel quietly and to drink the bitter tasting tea. He had tasted green tea before, but this particular tea seemed stronger. He tried to force back the frown that started to appear on his face with each sip.

After school, Masako drove Matt and his mom to the middle school. Matt slipped into one of the washrooms and changed into his track pants and a T-shirt. He noticed that all the toilets were traditional Japanese. He glanced about. No one else seemed to be around. This was as good a time as any, he figured, to try using one.

Anna Aoki had been right. It did remind him of an up-ended urinal lying there on its back. No big deal though. "Piece of cake," he mumbled a moment later, closing the door behind him. "Piece of cake."

As Matt met Masako and his mom back in the schoolyard, a dozen ball players dressed in full uniform burst through a set of double doors at the far side of the building. The uniforms were white with navy pinstripes on the pants and matching blue undershirts and caps. The players jogged onto the sandy playing field looking ready for serious play, shirts tucked neatly into their belted pants.

Matt drew his brows together into a frown. Maybe he wasn't going to get to play after all. "I thought this was just a practice today!"

"*Hai*," Masako stated. "Practice today. Practice every day. Two hours, after school."

Matt's blue eyes widened with wonder. "They practise everyday," he asked, "in full uniform?"

Masako nodded.

"Not in the wintertime," Matt stated matter-of-factly.

"Yes," she said. "Gym, in winter."

Matt's heart raced. His mind as well. Did Mr. Hart and Mr. Crowley know any of this? Did Mrs. Bartley? She might not have suggested a baseball game if she had known the Japanese were such diehards.

Mr. Ozaki waved Matt onto the playing field. Yoshi moved aside, making room for him to join the circle of players doing stretches.

When they began the jumping jacks, their voices rose in a loud chant. "*Ganbare! Ganbare!*"

"We say, 'Fight! Fight!'" Yoshi explained.

After the warmups, the team began a series of drills. Matt took his place with the others. Mr. Ozaki split the group into pairs. Immediately, Yoshi selected Matt as his partner. They lined up approximately twenty metres apart and tossed the ball back and forth, back and forth, lightly at first, then harder and harder. Backing up another twenty metres, they repeated the action. They moved farther and farther apart, their throws remaining hard and strong despite the incredible distance.

The players hustled from drill to drill with amazing enthusiasm and precision. Matt was mesmerized. These guys were good. They seemed to have a lot more energy than the players back home. That was the biggest difference. And they looked so professional, for a school team. They were more organized, more hyped, more into it, than even the East City Sharks. Sure, the Queen Elizabeth squad were decent ball players, but they didn't take their ball this seriously, and they didn't have real uniforms, just T-shirts. They were dead meat!

14

Besuboru

Supper that night was cooked right at the kitchen table, where thin strips of meat sizzled in a large round pan. There were several small bowls filled with a variety of vegetables nearby. It was fun cooking what you wanted right on the grill in front of you. And there was lots of time for conversation as everyone lingered around the table.

Matt quizzed Mr. Ozaki while his wife served as interpreter.

"You practise a lot for a school team," Matt said. "Our school team does not take ball nearly so seriously."

"Constant work allow great gain. Many years ago, Ministry of Education say baseball like martial arts, require timing, concentration, harmony in mental and physical strength."

Mr. Ozaki nodded as his wife translated.

"Baseball like *bushido*, the way of the samurai. *Bushido* code demand learning, skill, also loyalty, self-control, discipline and selflessness."

Matt smiled to himself. He had made the same connection while touring the Ninja temple. The whole idea of the samurai had made him think of his team, the East City Sharks. Matt told Yoshi and his father all about the Sharks, about their season last year and how they had battled it out with the Lakefield Lions. He explained to Yoshi that many of the Queen Elizabeth players also played for the Sharks.

"Ben won't be playing this year, though," Matt added sadly.

"Why?" Yoshi asked.

"We are a softball team. He wants to play hardball."

"Ahh," Yoshi nodded, smiling.

Matt brightened. "You should come to Canada. The team could use a good catcher."

Yoshi laughed.

Matt described the uniforms of the East City Sharks.

"Good colours," Yoshi stated. "Colours of red-crowned crane."

Matt suddenly furrowed his brow. "Why do you wear uniforms to practice?" he asked.

"Practice important," Mr. Ozaki replied. "For young players, more important than game."

"Yoshi is a good player," Matt added. He turned and addressed his friend. "Do you think you'll play in the pro leagues here someday?"

"Yes, yes," Yoshi replied enthusiastically. "I play baseball. Twelve teams in Japan," he explained. "Owned by big corporations." He was becoming more and more confident using English since spending time with Matt.

"Six, Central League; six, Pacific," Mr. Ozaki added.

"We cheer for Chunichi Dragons of Central League," Yoshi said. "Pennant winners meet, Japan Series. Teams work out all day, hot summer, too." He smiled as he continued, "Dad say, North Americans play ball; Japanese work at it."

"High school baseball very important," Masako added. "Win prefecture, go to national tournament. Tournament on television."

"Yoshi play soon," her husband added. "Needs to work hard."

Yoshi nodded.

"Maybe," Matt laughed, "you should take that red sun off the Japanese flag and put a baseball in the centre."

15

Chains of Cranes

Daiichi Middle School was much like Daiichi Elementary, only it had a large swimming pool and an electronic security system outside every classroom. A group of students performed the dragon dance in the courtyard area in front of the school to welcome the exchange students. Yoshi was one of them and he offered Matt a chance to try manoeuvering the huge red costume.

Upon entering the class, Yoshi hung a paper chain around Matt's neck. It was constructed of *origami* paper cranes in every colour of the rainbow. Each Canadian student received a similar chain of cranes.

"The Japanese crane is a symbol of long life and happiness," the teacher began, her lively dark eyes exuding warmth and friendliness. She was the English teacher at the middle school and spoke the language fluently. "It has also become a symbol of peace because of the story of Sadako. Have you heard the story of Sadako?" Most of the Canadians shook their heads.

"Every student from every country in the world should learn the story of Sadako and the Thousand Paper Cranes. It is not only a beautiful story, it is also a good example of the power of just one person to effect change."

The teacher had the Japanese students introduce their guests to the rest of the class, then push their desks to the side of the room and group the chairs in a circle. Pulling her chair into the cozy circumference she began to read:

> Sadako Sasaki was hospitalized for leukemia back in 1955 because of the effects of radiation from the bombing of Hiroshima in World War II. According to Japanese legend, cranes are said to live for a thousand years. One day a friend reminded her of the legend and suggested that if she folded a thousand paper cranes, the gods might grant her wish to be well once again. With patience and determination Sadako began folding. She made each crane from a square of paper in the ancient art of *origami*. Many people who visited brought special paper for her to fold. Some of her cranes were made out of candy wrappers, the smallest folded with the help of a toothpick.
>
> Before long more than six hundred cranes hung from the ceiling of the hospital room. With every crane she folded, this twelve-year-old girl wished for old age. She also wished for peace in the world so no more children would have to die because of war.
>
> Sadako never made it to a thousand. She folded her last one, her six-hundred-and-forty-fourth in October that year. Upon Sadako's death, her classmates folded three hundred and fifty-six paper cranes, so she could be buried with one thousand. They also told her story to the people of Japan by publishing her letters and writing. The people were so inspired that a monument was built in 1958 in Hiroshima's Peace Park to honour her and all children who had died as a result of the bombing. Young people throughout Japan helped collect the

money for the sculpture of Sadako holding a golden crane in her outstretched arms.

Sadako lives on in the hearts of the people who hear her story. Even today, thousands of children fold paper cranes and place them under the monument. Now, not just a thousand, but millions of paper cranes are placed beneath Sadako, each one folded by a young person hoping for peace.

The teacher quickly brushed a tear aside, then turned toward the Canadian students. "This is why the *origami* crane has become a symbol of peace, not only in Japan, but for all people of the world. This is why we present paper cranes to you today as a token of good will between Japan and Canada."

Matt sat quietly for a brief moment. The teacher had been right. It was a great story. It was all about loyalty and friendship and peace. Matt glanced over at Ben. It was ridiculous that such a stupid little thing had come between them. He kept wanting to put the blame on Ben, but he was the one who was mostly at fault. Maybe if the right moment came he could straighten things out. Hopefully, he would get a chance to do it before the baseball game.

16

We Gotta Have *Wa*

Before Matt had an opportunity to catch Ben alone, Kate approached Matt and Yoshi out on the schoolyard. It was shortly after lunch and the ball game was only a couple of hours away.

"Do you mind if I talk to Matt for a minute?" she asked Yoshi.

"It doesn't matter if Yoshi hears." Matt placed one hand on his friend's arm. "You want to talk about Ben, right?"

Kate nodded.

"Yoshi knows all about it. I told him last night."

"I decided," Kate began, "if Sadako can ..." She paused for a moment searching for the proper word. "How did the teacher say it?"

Matt stood silent, motionless.

"Effect change," Yoshi offered calmly.

"Yeah, that's it." Kate smiled at Yoshi. "That's what she said. If Sadako can effect change then maybe so can I." Kate's bright blue eyes pierced Matt's. "Remember last year how you were the one to get the Sharks back on track?"

"Yeah, right," Matt muttered stiffly. "Remember how I was the one that got us off track in the first place?"

"I know. I know. But you turned it around, and we had a great season. But," she added, her tone of voice becoming serious, "if we're going to have any hope of winning today, we gotta have *wa*."

"What are you talking about?" Matt asked.

"*Wa!*" Kate cried. "It's the Japanese word for team spirit and unity."

Yoshi nodded, approvingly.

Kate tossed her long hair and rolled her eyes. "You know how crazy my dad is about baseball?"

Matt nodded. Everyone knew how crazy Mr. Crowley was about baseball.

"Well, he even knows all about Japanese baseball. He follows the teams and their stats. He reads books about it. In fact, that's the title of one of his books, *You Gotta Have Wa.* Anyway," she continued, "Dad knows you and Ben haven't been too friendly lately. Everybody knows. It's not good for the team." Kate's eyes lowered and her voice softened. "It's not good for us either. We were friends. We were good friends. Remember how much fun we all had last year?"

Matt's shoulders relaxed and a smile began tugging at the corners of his mouth. "I've been wanting to apologize," he confessed. "It's just … It just seems like it's never the right time."

"Right now could be the right time," Kate exclaimed, "with all this talk of peace and harmony."

Matt looked at Yoshi.

Yoshi nodded. "Gotta have *wa*," he said, grinning broadly. "Lots," he chuckled, "to beat us."

Matt laughed. Then suddenly, his voice became serious. He looked at Kate. "I know, I know," he began. "I was thinking about it in the classroom. I was going to try and talk to Ben before the game. But will he want to talk to me?"

"Oh, yes!" Kate cried. "He really misses hanging out with you. I miss it too. Just because Ben and I are going out doesn't mean we all can't still be friends." She punched Matt playfully on the arm. "Guys just hate talking about this kind of stuff." Kate glanced in the direction of the school. "Actually he's waiting in the gym right now. I'll go get him for you if you like."

"Tell him," Matt began, his eyes scanning the schoolyard, "to meet me at the backstop in five minutes."

Kate and Yoshi walked back to the gym together.

Kate was right. Guys did hate this kind of stuff. She was also right that now was the right time to apologize, Matt decided, walking purposely toward the ball diamond at the far end of the yard.

The diamond was sand-covered, even the outfield. It was different from what he was used to, but at least he had fielded lots of balls at the practice here the night before. He had gotten a pretty good feel for how to play the bounces.

The bottom of the backstop was made out of cement, not wood like the backstops back at home. He stood there for a moment, daydreaming at home plate. It was hard to believe that in little more than an hour he would be standing at the plate playing ball in Japan. If anyone had told him that a year ago, he would have told them they were crazy.

Suddenly, before he even had a chance to practise his apology, Ben was there, standing beside him. "Kate said you wanted to talk to me."

Matt smiled sheepishly. He fumbled in his mind for a few seconds trying to find the right words. Finally, he blurted, "I'm sorry I was such a jerk."

Ben's round face broke into a huge grin. "So am I," he said. "I mean, not that you … that you're such a jerk, but that this whole thing happened."

Matt couldn't help but laugh. "Actually," he began, "I guess it's in the genes."

Ben looked puzzled.

"You know, the whole hardball thing. It seems to be a big Japanese thing. If you get really good at it, maybe someday you'll come and play ball in Japan."

"We're supposed to be doing that today. Remember? And we'd better get moving," Ben added. "We've still got to get dressed and Frank ..." He stopped to correct himself. "Coach Crowley wants us to warm up for at least forty-five minutes before game time, seeing how we haven't practised for ages."

Matt smiled. Not only had he practised the night before, but he was starting to feel pretty good — great in fact. It had been months since he and Ben had been friendly. The awkward feeling he had been experiencing around Ben now totally disappeared. There they were, joking around just like they always had.

Matt began jogging in the direction of the gym. It was amazing how much better he was beginning to feel. They might even have a chance to win this game, now that they had ... what had Kate called it? Ahh! *Wa!*

17

East Meets West

"Check out the opposition," Ben exclaimed, as the Japanese squad jogged onto the playing field. "Would you look at those uniforms?"

Matt nodded and smiled. He waved at Yoshi.

"Nobody told me we were going to the Olympics," Ryan blurted. Turning his cap around to face the front, he picked up his pace.

Steve and Mike both stopped dead in their tracks. Matt smiled again. He had experienced all this the night before. It was no longer intimidating to him. Maybe he should have warned the others. He glanced over at Kate. She smiled back at him, not the least bit flustered.

Matt studied the coaches. Mr. Crowley didn't seem fazed, but Mr. Hart was standing, jaw dropped, gaping. Quickly, he regained focus and called the outfielders aside in order to knock out a few fungoes. Mr. Crowley began working with the infield. First, they played a quick game of pepper, then he took over the bat and swatted several sharp grounders to each of them.

The coaches had decided the ball game would last seven innings, four innings of three-pitch and three of hardball. The Canadian team would provide the pitching for the three-pitch; the Japanese team would supply the hardball pitchers. It had taken a while to sort out a proper format, but eventually everyone agreed that this was a fair solution — approximately half the game Canadian-school style, the rest, Japanese.

Matt moved toward the plate. He was told a game of *jan ken poi* would determine who would take the field first.

"*Jan ken* what?" Matt questioned.

"Japanese game," Naigai explained. "*Jan ken poi*. You probably know it, but you say rock, paper, scissors."

Matt's eyes sparked with recognition. "Ben and I used to play this game — in church." He had not realized the game was Japanese.

Matt thought of choosing paper but at the last second changed his mind. Rock seemed harder, stronger, more substantial, like the ones he had seen in the gardens they had toured.

"On count of three," Naigai said. "*Ichi, ni, san.*"

No interpretation was necessary at this point. The hand gestures said it all — paper covers rock. Matt frowned. He had lost.

"Teams always bow to one another before a game," Ria instructed, waving the Queen Elizabeth team toward home plate.

Matt grinned up at Yoshi as he bowed. It was going to be hard to think of him as the opposition.

Moments later, the Japanese team charged onto the diamond, chanting loudly, "*Ganbare! Ganbare!*"

"They are saying, 'Fight, Fight!'" Matt explained to his teammates.

"Wow," exclaimed Steve, impressed. "You're really picking up the Japanese."

Mike jogged onto the mound. He was going to pitch for the three-pitch segment. Kate would fill in when it was his turn to bat.

Matt wondered what the Japanese team thought of Kate. There were no girls on their team. The younger Queen Elizabeth team had two girls — the Jackson sisters, Cassie and Rebecca. He would have to ask Yoshi about that later.

Mr. Crowley gathered his players for a pre-game huddle. "Don't let those uniforms throw you," he cautioned. "We're a good team too. We should do well in the three-pitch segment. They won't be used to this kind of pitching. And they won't be able to play their style of game — the sacrifice bunt, the squeeze play, that type of thing. If we work hard we should be able to carry a lead into the second half of the game."

The umpire, a medium-sized man dressed in a baby blue shirt, navy pants, mask and belly pad, motioned for Matt to approach the plate. Matt always batted leadoff for the Sharks, and Coach Crowley had slotted him in the familiar spot. He remembered to bow to the umpire like Ria had said, then gripped the smooth wooden bat in his hands, lining up his knuckles centre to centre the way Elaine, the batting instructor, had shown him the summer before. A twinge of excitement fluttered within him, but for the most part, he felt pretty relaxed. Was it because Mike's familiar face was there on the mound?

Matt took a few practice swings as he shuffled his feet into position. Mike pitched it in, trying his best to create a gentle arc that Matt could rip into. He did justice to the perfect pitch, smacking a hard-liner, arrow-straight, toward third. Simultaneously leaping and thrusting his glove into the air, the third baseman made the first out of the game look easy.

After firing the ball around the horn, the Daiichi squad tossed it back to Mike on the mound.

Ryan was up next. He let the first pitch go by, then took a good level cut at the second offering, smacking a single into shallow right field.

"Let's bring that runner home," Mr. Hart yelled to Steve, who was batting third.

Steve lobbed a soft fly into centre field. Two out.

"Shoot," stammered Ben, from the on-deck circle.

"Come on, Ben," shouted Matt encouragingly. "Touch gr ..." Matt caught himself just in time. He was going to say touch green, but there was no green here. If Ben could get good wood on the ball he might be able to knock Ryan in. Ben was a good hitter and Ryan was lightning on the base paths.

The visitors' bench cheered enthusiastically as the ball rose high off Ben's bat into deep left field. Matt was not nearly as expectant as the others. He had seen these fielders in action the night before and they had all been pretty fluid. The left fielder turned, angling his body to follow the ball, flawlessly gathering it in his outstretched glove.

The Queen Elizabeth squad raced onto the field smacking their well-worn gloves, chattering encouragingly to one another. The majority of players assumed the defensive positions they played for the East City Sharks. Ryan and Steve handled the heart of the infield, covering shortstop and second base. Kate played left field while Matt patrolled centre. Ben caught and Mike pitched and sometimes played first base. The two Retallick boys, Stephen and Shaun, and Daniel Mai, who all played church league ball, completed the lineup.

The leadoff batter for Daiichi caught nothing but air on the first swing. He ripped harder at the next one, undercutting the ball and popping it up to Steve at second. This is what Coach Crowley was talking about, Matt thought. The slower pitching style would keep the hitters off balance for a while.

Yoshi approached the plate. He was a good bunter, Matt had concluded after watching him at the practice. He would have to warn the infielders about that before the last half of the game. Yoshi, too, had problems adjusting his swing to the slower pace, missing the first pitch and pulling the final two into foul territory.

Kate caught the third out of the inning, chasing down a soft fly ball in shallow left.

"Three up! Three down!" chanted Matt racing in from centre.

The other fielders joined him. "Three up! Three down!"

The next two innings continued in much the same manner — the Daiichi team fielding flawlessly, but struggling at the plate. The Canadian team, however, managed a run in the top of the third. Mike's deep fly cashed Steve who, under Coach Crowley's direction, tagged up and scored.

Mr. Ozaki called his players into a quick huddle before the bottom of the fourth.

Coach Crowley took the opportunity to warn Matt and the others. "The honeymoon is over," he warned. "Everybody's had a look at the ball. They'll be onto the pitching now. Be on your toes out there!"

Daiichi's shortstop approached the plate. Shuffling his feet, he settled into position and waited patiently for the pitch. The batter swung, connecting smoothly, smashing a frozen rope into shallow centre.

Kazuki was up next. He screamed a hot grounder to Ryan on short. In one fluid motion, Ryan scooped it up, and tossed the ball to Steve, cutting off the lead runner.

The next batter hit a long fly ball into deep centre. Matt chased it down, caught it and pivoted, returning the ball quickly to the cut-off and hustling back into his defensive position. He had been a little nervous after that first hit, but now the butterflies were at rest. Although Kazuki stood on first, there were already two outs and one of the weaker batters was at the plate.

The small Daiichi right fielder popped the ball to Shaun Retallick, who was playing close to the line at third.

The three-pitch segment of the game was over and two of Daiichi's pitchers began warming up behind the screen. Yoshi caught for one, Ben the other. The school balls were softer and a little smaller than regular hardballs.

Again, Coach Crowley gathered his players. "We're in pretty good shape." He smiled proudly as he adjusted his cap. "We're right where we wanted to be. But," he cautioned, "we're going to have to focus to keep up the strong defence. You infielders be ready for a bunt." He quickly scanned the group looking to make eye contact with Mike Freeburn and Shaun Retallick. "Especially you guys on the corners."

"Especially when Yoshi's up to bat," Matt added.

"We'll be ready for 'em," Mike responded.

"When you're at the plate," Coach added, "remember, the Japanese strike zone is a little wider than ours. If it's close, you're swinging."

Amidst the cheering and banner waving of their fellow students, the Daiichi squad once again charged onto the field.

The first three Canadian batters went down in order while Daiichi gleaned a run in the bottom of the inning. The sixth inning was much the same. Ben grounded out, Daniel Mai and Steve Retallick both KO'd. Daiichi, however, collected two, Yoshi garnering both RBIs with a stand-up double.

The score was Daiichi 3, Queen Elizabeth 1.

Things were looking grim, Matt figured as he jogged off the field. Just let me get to bat, he told himself. He had hit this very pitcher at the practice the night before. There was no reason he couldn't do it here today. He smacked his fist into his mitt. His eyes narrowed in determination. He was going to get a hit!

Shaun Retallick led off the top of the seventh. He managed a foul tip on the first pitch but his swing was late. He worked the count to three and two, then watched the last one go by catching the outside corner.

"*Sutoraiku*," shouted the umpire.

To the surprise of the Japanese squad, Kate squared around on her first offering, laying down a perfect bunt in the direction of third. She scampered down the line, beating out the throw by half a step.

One out; one player on.

"C'mon, Mike. You can do it!" Matt hollered from the on-deck circle.

The bench took up the cheer. Mike worked the count to two and two before ripping a hard-liner up the middle. The pitcher jumped and caught the ball almost as if he'd known it was coming.

Two out; one on.

This was it, Matt told himself. It was up to him. He stepped up to the plate, butterflies fluttering once again. He exhaled. Pretend it's batting practice, he told himself. Relaxing his grip on the bat, he intentionally lowered his shoulders, releasing the tension, as the pitcher reeled back on the mound.

He let the first pitch go by.

Sutoraiku, gestured the umpire.

"Come on, Matt. You can do it!" shouted Ben from the bench. Matt smiled. It felt great to hear the good-natured chatter of his friend.

Matt ignored the next pitch as well.

"*Boru*."

"Good Eye," chanted his teammates. "G, double O, D, E, Y, E, Good Eye, Good Eye."

As the ball approached the plate for the third time, Matt shifted his weight to his back leg, then stepped smoothly forward into the pitch. It was perfect, over the very heart of the plate.

CRACK! The ball went soaring into the blue, cloudless sky. Matt did not pause to admire his hit. He tore toward first while the Canadian bench leapt to its feet, cheering wildly.

Kate was already rounding second, heading for third. Coach Crowley waved her on. Soon Matt was in the same position. He focussed on the coach.

"Keep going!" Coach shouted, left arm windmilling frantically. "Take home!"

Matt dug deep, trying to pick up his pace, trying his best to stretch the hit into a home run. Suddenly, there was Yoshi, poised to receive the ball. It was going to be close.

18

Play at Home

Matt didn't have time to reflect on the fact that his new friend was now his foe. His instincts took over. Arms thrusting, feet flying, the momentum of his slide carried him across home plate. Again, there was the tangle of arms, legs, dust and ball.

Matt stared up at the umpire. It had been close. Matt had felt the pressure of the glove when Yoshi applied the tag. It had felt like a tie. But what would the umpire's decision be? Whatever it was, Matt had to calmly accept it. They had all been warned by both Naigai and Ria not to talk back to the ump.

Suddenly, a small white sphere oozed slowly out of Yoshi's glove, coming to rest against the side of Matt's leg.

"Safe," the umpire called.

With the score now tied, the Queen Elizabeth team exploded into celebration.

Matt gazed up at Yoshi. Had the force of the tag knocked the ball out of his glove? Yoshi didn't seem upset or surprised. Was Matt imagining it, or was there a hint of a smile behind those dark brown eyes. Had he dropped the ball on purpose?

Matt stood, brushing himself off as his teammates clustered near the backstop. They all waited with outstretched arms in order to give Matt the customary round of high-fives.

Naigai and Ria were there too, and Masako. Masako handed him a small, colourful doll. "Japanese tradition," she explained, "when someone hits a home run in the big leagues."

Matt grinned from ear to ear. He glanced over at Yoshi. He was grinning too.

"Game's not over yet," Coach Crowley reminded them after Ryan popped out, ending the at bat. "We've got to play tight defence."

It was the bottom of the seventh, the bottom of the order too, Matt noticed, as the right fielder strode to the plate. Even so, the hitter drilled the second pitch through the hole between first and second.

The next batter squared around with the pitch, sending a soft dribbler toward first. Mike, expecting the play, barged bull-like down the line. He quickly turned and fired the ball to Steve covering at first.

The Daiichi fans chanted loudly as the third baseman left the on-deck circle. He worked the count to two and two, then stroked a hard grounder to Ryan on short. Ryan checked the nearby runner, then gunned the ball to first for the out.

Two out with a runner on second, Matt reminded himself, shifting his weight nervously. One more out to go. Suddenly, the ball was in the air. Matt moved toward it, but Kate called him off, making the last out of the game.

Matt raced off the field. Would there be extra innings he wondered? The odds of them holding the Japanese team scoreless for another at bat were pretty slim.

Coach Crowley was already addressing the situation. "We really should play one more inning," he told Mr. Ozaki, through an interpreter. "In fairness to your team. We did play four innings of three-pitch and only three of hardball."

"No, no, tie is good," Naigai explained, after conferring with the coach. "Very honourable way to end game. Perfect in fact. There are no losers."

She was right about that, Matt decided. The tie felt pretty good to him.

19

Making *Mochi*

Daiichi teachers, host families and the Canadian delegation gathered in the school library for a potluck farewell dinner that evening. Once again, the tables were beautifully arranged and well laden. There were many dishes Matt had not yet experienced. And he had a new appreciation for some of the items offered, like the watermelon on the fruit trays. He had noticed one in the grocery store the day before selling for two thousand yen. That was about twenty-eight dollars Canadian, he had figured.

Mrs. Bartley had been right. The Japanese were generous people. Matt had received numerous gifts that day as well. Not only the doll after his home run, but other gifts from the Ozakis, from their neighbours, from the school, from the town, even a tea cup from one of the school cooks.

After the main course, the school principal and another man hauled a large wooden drum into the centre of the room.

"For making *mochi*," Naigai explained. "It's the traditional way of preparing rice cakes. We usually do this on New Year's Day, but this is a special occasion."

Matt smiled warmly at the interpreter. It sure was.

Ria handed Matt and Yoshi the wooden mallets. As they took turns rhythmically hammering the rice into a smooth paste, Matt studied Yoshi's smile. He was still trying to figure out if his friend had dropped that ball on purpose. Mrs. Bartley's statement kept filtering through his mind. The Japanese were generous people. Were they that generous? Maybe some day Matt would ask Yoshi.

As it turned out, Matt did not particularly like the gooey texture of the small round cakes that were formed from the rice mixture, but it had been fun making them.

After everyone had finished eating, it was time for the farewell speeches.

It was the vice-principal's words that affected Matt the most. "It is by learning about worlds beyond our own borders that we gain an acceptance of one another and overcome our fear of experiencing the unknown."

He's right about that, Matt thought to himself. He had almost passed up on the chance to come to Japan because he had been unsure of trying something different. It was funny how everything had worked out. Everything he had worried about had turned out to be the exact opposite of what he feared — the flight, the food, the toilets. Even the baseball was not what he had expected.

It was in Japan that Matt had worked things out with Ben too. What had Ben said the day they had argued? That he wanted to try something different? Matt couldn't fault him for that. He really did hope it all worked out for him.

Too soon, it was time for the Canadian delegation to load the bus. Saying good bye was hard. Matt and Yoshi had become good friends and the Ozakis had been great hosts.

"You will always have a home here in Japan," Masako said as she hugged both Matt and his mom.

"And you are welcome to stay with us any time you want to come to Canada," Marg Tucker reciprocated.

Mr. Ozaki bowed and firmly grasped Matt's hand.

Yoshi stood looking at Matt. Matt hesitated. He didn't know if it was the proper thing but suddenly he found himself hugging Yoshi.

"Don't forget to e-mail me," Matt said later, stepping onto the bus.

"You, too," Yoshi replied.

"I'll be checking out the Japanese baseball web sites," Matt added. "To see how your Dragons are doing."

Matt, Ben, Kate, Ryan, Steve and Mike all crowded together at the back of the bus. They waved frantically through the rear window as it pulled away from Daiichi.

"*Sayonara*," Matt cried.

"*Sayonara*," Yoshi shouted. "*Sayonara*, Sharks!"

Other books you'll enjoy in the Sports Stories series ...

Baseball

☐ *Curve Ball* by John Danakas #1
Tom Poulos is looking forward to a summer of baseball in Toronto
until his mother puts him on a plane to Winnipeg.

☐ *Baseball Crazy* by Martyn Godfrey #10
Rob Carter wins an all-expenses-paid chance to be bat boy at the
Blue Jays spring training camp in Florida.

☐ *Shark Attack* by Judi Peers #25
The East City Sharks have a good chance of winning the county
championship until their arch rivals get a tough new pitcher.

☐ *Hit and Run* by Dawn Hunter and Karen Hunter #35
Glen Thomson is a talented pitcher, but as his ego inflates, team
morale plummets. Will he learn from being benched for losing his
temper?

☐ *Power Hitter* by C. A. Forsyth #41
Connor thought his summer would be a write-off when he was
sent to live with his baseball-crazed relatives in Winnipeg. That
is, it would have been a write-off if he hadn't discovered that he
had a secret talent.

☐ *Sayonara, Sharks* by Judi Peers #48
Ben and Kate are excited about the school trip to Japan, but Matt's
not sure he wants to go. Japan sounds a bit too different for him
— particularly the food and the toilets. He's also worried he'll
miss the tryouts for the Sharks softball team.

Basketball

☐ *Fast Break* by Michael Coldwell #8
Moving from Toronto to small-town Nova Scotia was rough, but
when Jeff makes the school basketball team he thinks things are
looking up.

☐ *Camp All-Star* by Michael Coldwell #12
In this insider's view of a basketball camp, Jeff Lang encounters some unexpected challenges.

☐ *Nothing but Net* by Michael Coldwell #18
The Cape Breton Grizzly Bears prepare for an out-of-town basketball tournament they're sure to lose.

☐ *Slam Dunk* by Steven Barwin and Gabriel David Tick #23
In this sequel to *Roller Hockey Blues*, Mason Ashbury's basketball team adjusts to the arrival of some new players: girls.

☐ *Courage on the Line* by Cynthia Bates #33
After Amelie changes schools, she must confront difficult former teammates in an extramural match.

☐ *Free Throw* by Jacqueline Guest #34
Matthew Eagletail must adjust to a new school, a new team and a new father along with five pesky sisters.

☐ *Triple Threat* by Jacqueline Guest #38
Matthew's cyber-pal Free Throw comes to visit, and together they face a bully on the court.

☐ *Queen of the Court* by Michele Martin Bossley #40
What happens when the school's fashion queen winds up on the basketball court?

☐ *Shooting Star* by Cynthia Bates #46
Not only is Quyen dealing with a troublesome teammate on her new basketball team, there's also trouble at home. Quyen is worried about her parents, who seem haunted by something that happened in Vietnam.

Figure Skating

☐ *A Stroke of Luck* by Kathryn Ellis #6
Strange accidents are stalking one of the skaters at the Millwood Arena.

☐ *The Winning Edge* by Michele Martin Bossley #28
Jennie wants more than anything to win a gruelling series of competitions, but is success worth losing her friends?

☐ *Leap of Faith* by Michele Martin Bossley #36
Amy wants to win at any cost, until an injury makes skating almost impossible. Will she go on?

Gymnastics

☐ *The Perfect Gymnast* by Michele Martin Bossley #9
Abby's new friend has all the confidence she needs, but she also has a serious problem that nobody but Abby seems to know about.

Ice Hockey

☐ *Two Minutes for Roughing* by Joseph Romain #2
As a new player on a tough Toronto hockey team, Les must fight to fit in.

☐ *Hockey Night in Transcona* by John Danakas #7
Cody Powell gets promoted to the Transcona Sharks' first line, bumping out the coach's son, who's not happy with the change.

☐ *Face Off* by C. A. Forsyth #13
A talented hockey player finds himself competing with his best friend for a spot on a select team.

☐ *Hat Trick* by Jacqueline Guest #20
The only girl on an all-boy hockey team works to earn the captain's respect and her mother's approval.

☐ *Hockey Heroes* by John Danakas #22
A left-winger on the thirteen-year-old Transcona Sharks adjusts to a new best friend and his mom's boyfriend.

☐ *Hockey Heat Wave* by C. A. Forsyth #27
In this sequel to *Face Off*, Zack and Mitch encounter some trouble when it looks like only one of them will make the select team at hockey camp.

☐ *Shoot to Score* by Sandra Richmond #31
Playing defense on the B list alongside the coach's mean-spirited son is a tough obstacle for Steven to overcome, but he perseveres and changes his luck.

☐ *Rookie Season* by Jacqueline Guest #42
What happens when a boy wants to join an all-girl hockey team?

☐ *Brothers on Ice* by John Danakas #44
Brothers Dylan and Deke both want to play goal for the same team.

Riding

☐ *A Way with Horses* by Peter McPhee #11
A young Alberta rider invited to study show jumping at a posh, local riding school uncovers a secret.

☐ *Riding Scared* by Marion Crook #15
A reluctant new rider struggles to overcome her fear of horses.

☐ *Katie's Midnight Ride* by C. A. Forsyth #16
An ambitious barrel racer finds herself without a horse weeks before her biggest rodeo.

☐ *Glory Ride* by Tamara L. Williams #21
Chloe Anderson fights memories of a tragic fall for a place on the Ontario Young Riders Team.

☐ *Cutting It Close* by Marion Crook #24
In this novel about barrel racing, a talented young rider finds her horse is in trouble just as she is about to compete in an important event.

☐ *Shadow Ride* by Tamara L. Williams #37
Bronwen has to choose between competing aggressively for herself or helping out a teammate.